THE BILLIONAIRES WILLED WIFE

SOME MEN GET CARS AND ACCOUNTS, BUT ALEX
GETS ISLA

H.S HOWE

D1712827

*This book is dedicated to our mother who believe you're
never too old to follow your dreams. She inspired us by going
back to collage at age fifty to become a nurse.*

THE GOLDWEN SAGA

The Billionaires Willed Wife is book 1 in the Goldwen Saga.
Stay tuned for book 2 The Will to Try coming 2021

*I*sla drove the expensive rental car down the side roads of her hometown. It had been a long time since she'd set foot in this state. One phone call and she had hopped on the first available plane to fly halfway across the country to see the man who wouldn't do the same for her.

She kept replaying the message in her head—a hit and run, no doubt by a drunk driver. Her father had been working late, which wasn't unusual and therefore didn't result in concern when he didn't arrive at home at a reasonable hour. After all, what he did was nobody's business, and the staff was well trained not to ask questions. If the school bus hadn't spotted his car in the ditch the next morning, there was no telling how long he could have been out there, broken and bleeding from his head injury. Now he was damaged beyond repair with irreversible, catastrophic brain stem damage—a diagnosis that rendered him legally dead and put his living will into motion.

She'd been shocked to hear Alex's voice after all these years, and she still wasn't sure how he'd gotten a hold of her personal cellphone number. Alex, she remembered with a shiver then gripped the steering wheel and scolded herself. Now was not the time to think about him. She had to focus.

Ten years ago, she'd left this place and her family behind. Back then, she'd been determined to make it as an artist, a career her father had told her wasn't for women. He'd never supported any of her hobbies and often told her she wouldn't make it. He had predicted she would return before the year ended. That had only fueled her resolve to make something of herself and to become far wealthier than even her father.

Of course, that hadn't happened. Turned out, Dad was right about one thing; she wasn't skilled enough to make it in the art world. After all, she'd been classically trained, and though she could paint a sunset that could take one's breath away, it wasn't appreciated where she'd landed. It was all about abstract art in the big city, and she neither understood that kind of art nor had talent in it.

She'd met so many great people along the way, many neglected children, and thus changed career paths. Her ability to relate to lost and tormented souls made her a great therapist. So she had worked to put herself through college and was still paying off the student loans. It had all been worth it; the strength and happiness she found in her new life had stopped her from pursuing revenge.

For the past several years, she'd been content. She no longer missed the so-called finer things in life. Now here she was, throwing it all away.

As she wound down the long, curvy driveway and parked, she realized she was taking several hundred steps backward.

The only good news to come from the phone call was when she had learned her father had divorced the gold digger who'd "helped raise" her. That piece of information quite pleasantly surprised Isla. She actually smiled as she shut her door and approached the stone patio.

The place was like walking into a museum with priceless artwork hanging on the walls, along with other countries' artifacts. Her father was many things, but tasteless wasn't one of them.

Her high heels echoed across the marble floors. Looking around, she knew she wouldn't find one speck of dust, not if the staff respected both their job and dignity. She remembered the time her toddler brother had gotten into the baby powder. Her dad had fired her favorite nanny that day due to the handprint her stepmother had found on the hallway window.

The staircase gleamed in rich red wood and gloss, and overhead, the chandelier glittered as the bulbs hit every gemstone just right. Burgundy velvet curtains hung, showcasing the stained-glass window that once held a family of four portrait. She eyedt it curiously, as it was now a landscape without people.

She took the gray runner down the long hallway, remembering every fight, every tear, every internal cry she'd yelled while inside these four walls, until she reached the master suit.Isla crept slowly to the bedroom door, fully aware of what was on the other side. Anxiety and dread filled her. She'd used the slow stroll through the house like memory lane, but now she had no choice but to face her father head on. She contemplated another escape but knew the time had come—it was time to face the demons from her past.

"Daddy?" she said, opening the door. There was no way for him to answer, but nonetheless, she said it as a question, as if expecting him to say, 'Come in.'

The floorboards creaked as she stepped on each one, edging closer to the man in front of her. She watched the steady rise and fall of his chest, thanks to the monitors and tubes keeping him alive. Looking closely, she couldn't help but think this wasn't the same man who haunted her dreams.

Isla traced her fingers over the silk sheets, inching closer and closer as she zoomed in on his pale, lifeless face.

"They tell me you're gone," she whispered to him. "That you no longer hear or feel anything. They want me to make a decision, to pull the plug and let you go or to send you to a nursing home with twenty-four-hour care." She silently cursed herself for the tear that ran down her face. "The decision would be easier if *I* knew whether you were in pain."

A LOUD NOISE downstairs jolted her from her trance, and she debated whether she should hide or show her face.

Before she could decide, her brother entered—rthe only person in the world who had a right to hate her father as much as she did. Unfortunately, she feared he was just as big a snake as their dad. They hadn't bonded as children or adults; instead, they were constantly in some sort of sibling rivalry that usually resulted in one or both of them in tears or deep, deep trouble.

"Hello Isla," he drawled with a sick smile. His breath reeked of alcohol, and, for a moment, she was frozen in time. "Did you come to pull the plug on dear ole dad?" He inched toward her.

"You realize it's only two o'clock in the afternoon, right? Is there a reason you need to be three sheets to the wind at this hour?"

"It's five o'clock somewhere," he replied with a sinister grin.

"Charming." She rolled her eyes.

"What are you even doing here? You should know you won't see a cent of his money. He wrote you out of the will years ago," he slurred.

It was just what she needed to wake her up, and she dodged out of his way before he could get to close.

"Nah, I think I'll keep him alive in one of those high-priced homes. Make sure he uses up all the money in his accounts before I let him go." She shot him her own snakelike smile.

"You've always been a spontaneous little thing, dear sis. That's exactly why he's leaving you nothing—no access to his accounts and no control over his future." He stumbled forward, only air between them. "The decision is mine, and the decision is made. Kiss him goodbye while you have the chance." He spun around and darted from the tension-filled room, leaving Isla in question as to whether her dad even deserved her goodbye.

Unsatisfied, she soon raced down the steps after him. "Nice try, Daniel. Do you think his lawyer would have called me if the decision was yours?" As if on cue, she saw the very man in question walk through the front door. Her breath stuttered, and her walking slowed. It'd been just as many years since she'd seen Alex, the man her father had promised her to—tall, dark, sexy, and pure evil..

"Good, you're both here," Alex said in his deep, sexy voice. "I have a few forms for the two of you to sign. Have you made your decision, Isla?"

Her shoulders stiffened when his eyes locked on hers. "I want to put him in a home for as long as his money will allow," she replied, sounding more confident than she felt.

"If your goal is to drain his accounts, you'll be waiting a long time. He could live another hundred years and still have money left over," Alex informed her.

From the corner of her eye, she saw Daniel grin like the slim he was. The room suddenly felt as though it were closing in on her, cornered by two men who left scars that ran deep into her past. "I need air." Isla sighed faintly.

"I'll join you. After all, we have some catching up to do." Alex gestured to the door, awaiting her escape so he could follow her into the dark night.

"Please don't." She raised her hand as she sped past him and out the door. Gripping the railing, she inhaled a deep breath of cold air. This couldn't be happening.

"Don't let him get to you," Alex said, invading her personal space. "He's lying. He's not getting any more than you are, and that's of course if you both follow your father's carefully laid out plans"

"Ah, how exciting," she said dryly.

"The money is to be split equally between both of you, provided you both marry the person he has assigned to you and you produce an heir. After all, he doesn't want his legacy to end. You'll get one third of your inheritance after the wedding, the second third after the birth of a child, and the final sum on your five year anniversary. If one of you should choose to remain unwed, the other will get the full balance, and, if you both refuse, it will go to his ex wife, Janice."

She wanted to vomit. He was such a sick, twisted bastard. Her father had to know she wouldn't want either her brother or his mother getting their filthy hands on what they always wanted. He'd dealt his hand wickedly, knowing she didn't want the money but also knowing her hatred wouldn't want them having it either.

"And let me guess," she spat. "You're the lucky groom he has in mind?" The sick bastard must really be enjoying this.

"It just so happens that I am."

She couldn't breathe. She needed to get out of here and take time to process. Her feet moved automatically, but, as she went to pass him, he reached out and grabbed her arm.

"Isla—"

"Don't touch me!" she screamed, and he released her. "Don't you dare touch me." She made it past and into the safety of her car only to scream in frustration. Her keys, cellphone, and purse were all still inside. Nothing sounded better at that moment than laying her head on the steering wheel and crying.

*a*fter half a dozen deep breaths later, Isla heard a knock on her window.

Alex stood just outside her door, dangling the keys.

Isla closed her eyes and mentally braced herself to face his taunts about her desperation to escape. She took one last deep breath and rolled down her window. "Thank you, I'll take those." She swiped to grab them from him.

Alex stepped backward. "Not so fast. There's more we need to discuss."

"What else could there possibly be? This situation is impossible! Either I spend five years of hell married to a man who nearly destroyed me and give birth to his child, or I let my arrogant brother and his parasite mother gloat as they blow through the money my father was too busy earning to acknowledge what they were doing to me."

"Just give me an hour. Come to dinner with me, and afterward, I'll hand over your keys."

Isla hesitated. Her mind raced. As much as she didn't want to be around Alex, she was not looking forward to facing the demons in her own head once she was alone to process the blow she had just been dealt. "One hour. At Lucille's Diner. You're buying. And you will give me my keys now, because there's no way in hell I'm getting in a car with you."

"No such luck, sweetheart. Can't have you running off on me." Alex tucked her keys into his snug pocket.

Though she didn't want to, really didn't want to, she looked.

"I see I have your attention." Alex flexed his hips in her direction.

Isla scowled at him while trying to stop the flood of memories of wild passion, of pleasure like she'd never known before or since, memories she had long blocked out. "Just trying to decide how desperate I am to get my keys back. Nice to know your ego hasn't changed at all." Making her decision, she swung open the door, hitting him in the process. "Let's get it over with, Mr. Jones."

"Mr. Jones?" He raised an eyebrow. "Is that anyway to address the man who tasted and plucked your sweet little cherry?"

She slapped him hard across the face. "You disgust me!" She all but spat at him.

His long, firm fingers caught her wrist and pulled her body into him. "I do believe you *wish* that were true," he growled mere inches from her mouth.

"It is true!" she insisted, as much to herself as to him. "I knew this was a bad idea." She pulled away and began walking toward the building.

"Where do you think you're going?" he snarled.

"To find my phone so I can get an Uber. I told you I'm not getting in a car with you. And now I'm not going to listen to your blather. I'm not the same person I used to be. You will *not* control me."

"Oh, darling, I think we both know I was never the one in control." He scooped her up and tossed her over his shoulder.

She pounded on his back. "Dammit, Alex!"

"Stop all shouting, Isla. You're giving the neighbors quite a show." He smacked her playfully on the butt then tossed her onto the passenger seat.

"You're such an ass. No wonder Daddy loved you," she said, barely keeping her voice level.

"Don't ever compare me to him," he warned darkly.

"Ah, that's right. You never did care for the truth, did you?"

"That's enough, woman!" He slammed her door shut and stalked to the driver's side door. "I'm trying to help you, God knows why I bother!"

"Oh, thank you, Alex. My hero," Isla mocked.

"Dammit, Isla! I said, enough!" He violently shifted into gear, and the tires screeched as he pulled out of the lot.

Isla squeezed her fingernails into her palms, trying her best to stay calm. All she wanted to do was cry or scream, but she needed to keep her cool. One hour, just one hour then she could have her meltdown. There had to be a loophole; she'd get a second opinion. Alex couldn't be trusted. Obviously, he would suggest the marriage; it would make him filthy rich.

Her thoughts were interrupted when they pulled into the restaurant parking lot.

"Isla, please, can we just call a truce and be civil for the remainder of the night? Believe it or not, I do actually want to talk to you. Civilly."

"Only because I don't want to embarrass myself. I'm not doing it for you." She opened her door and walked in without waiting for him.

Alex watched her enter and wondered what he'd gotten himself into. He never could think straight around Isla, and it was clear that hadn't changed. He sighed and headed into the restaurant.

Slipping the hostess, a few bills he managed to get them a private booth.

"Don't you at least want to know who your father has in mind for Daniel?" he asked once they were alone.

"As if it matters, he'll do whatever it takes to get his hands on that money. He's like you in that aspect." Alex slammed a fist on the table at her words then raised her hands in surrender. "Civil. Sorry. Okay, I'll bite. Who is she?"

"Do you remember Anna Henderson?"

Isla gasped. "The farmer's daughter from down the road? The one who shoved him in the manure pit when they were in high school?"

Alex grinned. "That's the one."

"But Daddy hated that farm," she said more to herself than anything.

"Yes, but that was because of the smell. He admired the hard work and effort it took to run it. He also thought Anna would whip his son into shape. Despite what you think you know, you missed out on a lot of changes these past ten years."

Isla huffed. "And thank god, because the first twenty were a real shit show."

Alex's face softened. "I know. I know what they did to you. And, despite what you think, your father came to realize what he did to you as well."

Isla's anger flared. "So, he thought he would give the knife one final twist?"

The waitress approached their table and presented a bottle. "Would you care to sample the house wine? It pairs great with our cranberry sauce salmon."

"Fine," Alex said with a flip of his wrist. "And bring us a

fruit tray with chocolate sauce," he instructed with a dismissal tone.

She poured the wine, waited for the approval then left them alone once again.

"Isla, my feelings for you haven't changed. I wanted to wed you ten years ago, and I want to marry you now."

"Good thing dear old Dad isn't dead yet. Gives me time. "

"You're not really going to keep a vegetable, are you?"

Isla stared at the table in silent shock. Marriage? Was he insane? She eyed Alex, frowning. "I ... I ... I just don't know. I hate him," she whispered. "But I'm not a monster. And I don't feel I have enough information to make a life-or-death decision."

Alex slid a hand across the table to grasp her. "Isla, he's gone. I can give you all the proof and expert opinions you need."

His touch felt nice, oh so nice. Thank god the waitress chose that moment to arrive with the fruit. She had to get out of here. With her stomach in knots, there was no way she could eat. She swallowed hard. "Alex ... Please, just don't touch me."

After a moment's hesitation, he released her hand and beheld her. The blatant pain and misery on her face made him ache to take her into his arms and reassure her. But he thought changing the subject was likely safer for now. "Okay. No touching, for now. Please eat some fruit. I know how you get when you're stressed. I bet you haven't eaten all day."

"Don't pretend to know me, Alex. On the contrary, when I got the news, I celebrated at IHOP with all-you-can-eat pancakes. I had breakfast and lunch there." She was lying of course, but that was none of his business.

"Pancakes? Then why did I spend all those mornings making you French toast?" he asked, knowingly.

Her cheeks flamed. "Guess I lost the taste for them."

"Or perhaps no one has prepared them quite like I can—shirtless, with mounds of butter and fresh maple syrup," he said with a twinkle in his eyes.

"No, I don't think that's it." She shrugged. "I always have fresh maple syrup and shirtless men on hand."

Alex's nostrils flared, and his gaze narrowed. The idea of Isla in another man's arms, in his bed, made him want to punch a hole in the wall. No matter how long it had been, she was *his*. He shoved the plate at her. "Just eat the fruit, Isla."

Isla saw the darkness in his eyes and decided a strawberry with some chocolate wouldn't kill her, even if eating was not appealing in the slightest right now. She took a nibble. It was good. Better than good. Juicy, perfectly ripe and sweet, in exquisite contrast to the rich, dark chocolate sauce accompanying it. She sipped her wine and closed her eyes in a moment of appreciation for the pale liquid she hadn't been able to afford in years. "*Mmm*, delicious," she all but moaned, forgetting herself momentarily.

"And the woman says no touching," Alex muttered. Suddenly, his pants were a little too tight.

Her eyes snapped back open, and he loosened his tie. "It's just been a while," she explained. Oh, wrong thing to say she realized as he grinned. "Since I've had wine of this caliber,'" she quickly amended.

"With a moan like that, sounds like you've been going without more than just good wine."

Thank god for the waitress with the world's best timing. Before she had to dig herself from the hole she was in, their fish arrived. Though she mainly picked at her food, Alex managed to finish his entire plate and most of the fruit. She was ready for this meal to be over and was relieved when the bill arrived.

Reluctantly, Alex reached for his wallet. Unlike Isla, he wasn't ready for the evening to end. Before he could make an excuse to stall, she slipped from the booth.

"I need to visit the ladies room real quick. I'll meet you outside."

He nodded and watched her go. Silently, he prayed she would listen to reason. He wanted her back by his side where she belonged.

Isla slid into the passenger seat and buckled up. She mentally cursed herself for not grabbing her purse before they left. Her phone would be a nice distraction; the silence was suffocating, and she could smell him so clearly—that thick, sexy scent that only belonged to him.

"Thank you for accompanying me," Alex said, breaking the silence.

"You don't thank someone after abducting them, Alex."

He grinned and, well, it was contagious. Soon they were both laughing, but, as they rode into view of the house, she began to cry instead. He parked the car and unbuckled them both then slid her into his arms. For once, she didn't fight him and, instead, relaxed in his embrace and sobbed.

"He's gone, Alex. He's really gone. I'll never yell at him again. I'll never be able to curse in his face and demand answers." She panted between cries.

"Shh," he hushed, rubbing her back in a soothing motion. He held her until the sobs subsided then lifted her chin and wiped her cheeks. She shivered in his arms, and he brushed a thumb over her lower lip. God, how he missed her taste. But now wasn't the time or place. If he kissed her now, she'd run, and he'd have to live with the guilt.

"Let me drive you to where you're staying, Isla."

But she shook her head and pulled herself off his lap. "No, we had a deal, and I'm okay to drive." Holding out her hand, she met his gaze and, finally, he placed her keys in them.

"You're right. A deal is a deal. I won't push you. But, before you go, I need to let you know I think I have a way we can do this."

"Sure, let's just get married and get busy making babies."

"Clearly, you're not in the right frame of mind to hear what I have to say. You have my number. When your curiosity demands to know how to beat your father at his own game, get ahold of me." Before she could respond, he quickly exited and circled the car to open her door. He bowed mockingly. "Your freedom awaits, milady."

Silently, slowly, Isla rose from the car. She refused to give Alex the satisfaction of asking. "And not a moment too soon."

"Good to see you again, Isla," Alex taunted. "Don't forget to let me know what you decide about your father."

3

*E*ntering her father's room, she barely made it through the door before the stench of perfume assaulted her. No. No, no, no. Please not today, Satan.

But her silent pleas were unanswered as her stepmother turned to see who was there. Her throat closed. Speech was impossible, as every fiber of her being screamed, *Run!*

Janice had no such struggles. Her lips curled smugly. "I never thought I would be happy to see you. But then, I never envisioned you would be the one to ensure I inherited your father's fortune." She scrutinized Isla. "My, don't you look like something the cat dragged in. Looks like someone has been regretting her decision to rebel."

Isla's head snapped back; her spine went rigid. "I regret nothing. Except, perhaps, not reporting you for leaving Daniel and I unattended while you were off bingeing."

Janice's face reddened and twisted with rage. "You always were an ungrateful brat. Everything your father and I bought for you, and it was never enough. You were never satisfied. And I was entitled to self-care! My husband neglected me, and I was expected to behave like you were equal to Daniel. I bore him a son to pass on his name, and he barely noticed."

"You starved me for six years! Feeding my breakfast and dinner to your dog!"

"Please, I knew you were stuffing your face at school. Honestly, Isla, I did it for your own good. Nobody wants to marry a fat girl, not even Alex. Well …" she smiled cruelly. "That's not exactly true, is it? How much was your dowry? The millions tend to blur together for me. I never thought he cared about me, but he was clever in designing his will. He made it look like he was going to give you and Daniel his fortune, but he made the conditions such that neither of you could possibly succeed, ensuring you couldn't fight to keep me from inheriting."

Isla saw red. Blind with hatred, she heard herself say, "Oh, but that's where you're wrong, dear stepmother. Alex and I went to dinner last night. He wants to marry me. And I can think of worse things than being paid to marry an attractive man and having his baby. Besides, I can't wait to see Daniel's face when he realizes he won't get a cent. I think he thought he would still get money from you if I refused, and he didn't have to make up the way he treated Anna years ago."

"Please, Isla, you're a terrible liar. Alex might be willing to marry you for the money, but the two of you will never have a child or stay together for five years."

"It can't be that hard, considering you did it."

"Oh, darling, please. I'm a real class act, hosting and marriage are in my breeding. Sadly, you fought every etiquette class we ever enrolled you in." Janice shook her head.

"I hardly call Weight Watchers etiquette." Isla rolled her eyes.

"I was referring to piano and ballroom dancing. All these years later and you're still a hopelessly lost cause. "

"You never let me practice piano with smacking my hand with a ruler every time I made a mistake. And your dance teacher was a pervy old man with wandering hands." Isla felt bile rise in her throat at the memory.

"Had you been a proper lady, you have known how to handle those situations."

"Oh, I think I handled it just fine with a knee in the groin and my fist in his face," she snarled.

"To be fair, I rather enjoyed that too. Your father was clever in your punishment for that one."

"He sent me to a six-week, all-girls dance academy, which was far better than getting molested and dealing with you."

Janice rolled her eyes. "So dramatic."

"I fainted the first week due to overexertion and was treated for anorexia."

"Well, that's enough memory lane for me. I believe you came here to finish off your father. I'll leave you to it." Janice glided past her.

"You know why you never liked me, Janice? It's because you could never be me, and you could never beat me."

"We're family, Isla. I don't have to like you. I simply have to politely tolerate you in public." She sashayed down the stairs, leaving Isla and her father alone.

The day wasn't even half over, and she was already exhausted. Sinking into the rocking chair beside her father's bed, she squeezed her eyes shut, willing the bitter memories to fade.

A sound at the door had her opening her eyes. Alex leaned in the doorway, watching her. "How about I take you to lunch?"

18

She removed her gaze from his. "Why are you always trying to feed me?"

"You know I never like it when you skip a meal."

"Don't worry, I've already eaten today."

He raised a skeptical eyebrow. "The doctor is en route. I wasn't sure you'd want to be here when he arrived."

Isla gripped the armrests. "You're right. I don't want to be here. However, I *need* to be here. There's a one percent chance he'll start breathing on his own. It's small, but it's still a chance, and I need to be here to see it with my own eyes."

He nodded and proffered a brown leather lunch sack. "I thought you might say that, so I brought you a sandwich. Peanut butter and jelly, best comfort food known to date. There's a hot Thermos of coffee and a chocolate no-bake cookie as well." When she didn't move, he straightened, grabbed a chair he positioned beside her and opened the bag.

She raised a hand. "Alex, please, I'm not hungry."

He took the opportunity to link his fingers with hers. "That's the best part about comfort food, you don't have to be hungry to eat it." When she opened her mouth to further argue, he stuck a bite of thick homemade bread in her mouth.

She moaned, chewed and swallowed, then opened her mouth again so he could feed her another bite. He obliged, and her stomach growled, revealing the truth that she hadn't yet eaten today.

Alex ignored the sound and tore the sandwich into bite-sized pieces and fed it to her. The left side corner of her mouth had a small dab of jelly on it, and he wiped it away with his thumb. The contact had her catching her breath, and he held her gaze as he lifted his thumb to his mouth and sucked the sweet jam off it.

Her mouth fell open, and he moved in. "Alex," she whispered.

19

"Shh ..." He cupped her face in his hands and leaned in, touching their foreheads.

"Well, well, what do we have here?" Daniel asked from the doorway, breaking the spell.

"It's called human emotion, Daniel. You should try it sometime," Isla retorted. "Alex was being a gentleman and comforting me."

"What do you need comforting for? Knowing you'll never see a cent of Father's estate?"

"Knowing I can never tell him what a favor he did for me by giving me the peace of mind that you'll never inherit."

Daniel laughed sardonically. "Oh, I'll inherit. Even if Anna is too bullheaded to see the light, my mother will ensure I want for nothing."

"You wouldn't be able to handle having your mommy controlling you with the money, you'll lose your mind. But she won't be inheriting either."

Daniel looked angry, his voice low. "My mother might be a controlling witch, but you can't do anything about her inheriting. Unless your plan is to let Father live on the ventilator until pneumonia takes him in a few months, which only delays the inevitable. It doesn't change the will."

Isla felt her temper boiling over, and good sense went out the window. She couldn't let Daniel win! "Alex and I reconciled last night. He wants to marry me. I've come to see that Father's will was a blessing in disguise. He made sure I was reunited with Alex and provided for, for the rest of my life, while giving me the satisfaction of knowing my happiness cost you yours."

Daniel's face went white then beet red. "I don't believe you! You two hate each other!"

"Love and hate are two sides of the same coin. And we

THE BILLIONAIRES WILLED WIFE

were very happy together before. Why couldn't we be again?"

"It's true, Daniel," Alex inserted smoothly. "Isla and I will begin wedding planning as soon as the burial is complete."

"We were going to wait, but, well, I guess the cats of the bag." Slipping her mother's diamond from her pocket, she revealed the ring.

Daniel's jaw dropped.

"I believe that's my job, darling." Alex took the ring before she slid it on. "I know I promised you a big flashy proposal, but I don't see why we can't make it official here with your father present." Taking a knee, he proffered the ring. "Isla Renea Goldwen, I have loved you from the moment I first laid eyes on you."

Daniel made a gagging sound from across the room.

"I know I broke your trust all those years ago but know I look forward to making it up to you for the rest of our lives."

"More like the next five years," Daniel interjected.

"Will you make me the happiest man alive and marry me?" He raised the ring closer to her body.

She nodded, tears in her eyes.

Daniel clapped, mocking them. "Well, she is giving you a billion reasons to be happy. Guess she costs more with age."

"Are you sure you want to marry into this family?" she teased. "It comes with a few jackasses" She nodded toward Daniel.

"I'm sure. I don't plan to lose you a second time." He slid on the ring fully, aware she hadn't actually said yes.

"You're a good actress, sis, but not a great one. I'm not buying it," Daniel said through thinly veiled rage. "If you're so in love, why don't you go ahead and give him a kiss?"

"You're a known sex addict, Daniel. I don't think it would

be wise to get you worked up. We're pretty passionate," she said, trying to get in a dig while maintaining her boundaries with Alex.

But Daniel grinned his sick, knowing grin, and she had to grit her teeth and pretend not to notice. "Enjoying sex and being an addict are two very different things, dear sis. If you can go long spells without it, perhaps you should find a new partner and find out what all the raves are about."

"Nonsense," Alex told her, as if Daniel hadn't spoken. "Sex addiction is a disease usually brought on by a lack of ever experiencing real love and connection. He's never seen nor experienced real love, not from his parents and certainly not from any relationship. Therefore, I believe it is our duty to show him, and what better time than now?" He encircled her in his arms and knew she would protest yet again, but good ole Daniel helped him out.

"Go ahead, sis. Show me what I've been missing." He snickered.

So, she did. Though she thought acting like the perfect little fiancée might kill her, she had done this to herself. And all to get a rise out of him. Little did he know, in this moment, he was actually winning.

Alex lowered his mouth to hers and teased it until she moaned and shuddered in his arms. God yes, this, this is what had been missing in his life. He deepened the kiss, and she ran her hand through his hair just like old times, and he growled.

4

A voice cleared in the doorway, reminding him where they were. "Mr. Jones," the doctor inquired. "I have a few legal documents we need to review so we can proceed. May I have a moment alone with you in the hallway?"

Alex reluctantly released Isla and stepped out, shutting the door.

"Well played, sis," Daniel said, sauntering toward her.

She was so focused on the tingling in her lips that she didn't realize until it was too late that he'd backed her into a corner.

"I always knew you had it in you to whore yourself out for money. Remember that time I let Jimmy Andersen sneak into the bathroom while you were showering and take those photos of you?" He placed his hands on the wall just above her head.

"How could I forget? Those photos ended up all over the school, and I got blamed for it. Father sent me away to a nunnery for three months," she spat.

But he only grinned wider. "Well, let's just say I have no

problem believing you can snag a husband despite your dull personality."

"Well, thanks, bro. I'll take that as your prenuptial blessing given you yourself have finally stated you believe Alex will marry me," she said with a tight smile.

"I said you could get a husband. I didn't say I believed you could keep one. My guess is you're quite drab in bed, at least that's the word around town." It wasn't, of course, but he just had to needle her.

"You're sick. Hard to believe we share the same DNA," she fired back, knowing he was just goading her.

"Are you sure, Isla? Were you ever tested? Because I was, and there's a ninety-nine-point-nine percent chance he is my father."

"Guess he trusts my mother more than yours."

He raised his hand to her.

"Oh, please do it, Daniel. Give me a reason to press charges. We aren't children anymore. You won't be able to pass off the bruises you inflict on me as an accident. Not to mention Anna won't want to marry a criminal."

Clenching his fist, his eyes spit fire at her. "I guess I'll have to find new ways to hurt you then, won't I?" He lowered his hand and clutched her chin.

"Don't fucking touch me!" She knocked away his hand.

"Or what?" He gripped her chin firmer.

"*Alex!*" she screamed, knowing she was no match for Daniel. She trembled and hated that he knew exactly what button to push.

"Big mistake, sis." He stepped backward before the door opened.

Alex barreled through the door at the sound of pure fear in Isla's voice and rushed to her. "What is it?" She was visibly shaken, and he silently promised to never leave her alone in a room with her brother ever again. He should have known better.

"N-NOTHING. I JUST MISSED YOU."

He pulled her in and felt her shake with tension. "Don't worry, Isla. I'll never go far."

"Can we get out of here?"

Alex saw the anxiety on her face, but she would have to wait. "Not yet. We need to stay while they turn off the ventilator."

Isla closed her eyes. The idea of watching her father struggle to breathe and knowing it was her doing did not sound appealing at all. But she knew Alex was right. "Okay. When do we do that?"

"The doctor is here and ready as soon as you and Daniel say your goodbyes."

Daniel answered first. "I've got nothing to say to that traitorous bastard. Rot in Hell."

Isla frowned. "I would like a chance to speak to him. Alone."

"As you wish. Daniel, let's step into the hallway," Alex said firmly to avoid argument. Alex wanted to know what Daniel had done to get Isla so upset anyhow.

"SO ... WE MEET AGAIN." Isla pulled a chair to the side of his bed and sat. "I must have gone over what I'd say to you a thousand times, but now that the moment's here, it feels all wrong." She reached for his hand and squeezed it. "Can you feel that? Are you there?"

She blew out a breath as tears burned her eyes. "I have so

many questions, so many accusations and demands, and you're supposed to be here to answer to every one of them."

Tears fell, and her misery boiled. She didn't want to cry; he didn't deserve her pain. "Why did you do this to me? Why?" She gripping his hand harder than she should have and shook his arm. "Why didn't you love me? Why did you have to blame me for my mother's death? I loved her too. I needed her. I know you must have missed her, but had you ever taken the chance to get to know me, I could have softened the blow. I'm nothing like you, which tells me I must take after her. Would it have killed you to let me know? You hold all the memories and all I got was a photo and this wedding ring." Raising her hand, she showed him where it glittered on her fourth finger.

"And now I'm getting married. To the man you chose, a man you knew would never love me. Why was it your dying wish to leave me with eternal suffering? Didn't I give you exactly what you wanted? I left. You're most expensive problem left. No more reminders, no more attitude. You were home free. With me out of the picture, you finally had the perfect societal family."

She released his hand and squeezed the side of the bed in frustration. "And why, why did you divorce her? What did she do to you? You never cared what she did to me. She did her best to destroy me, and you let her. Do you have any idea the length of time it has taken me to block those memories so I could move on and find happiness? And just when I think I've succeeded, just when I'm the happiest I've ever been, you find a way to drive the knife right back in me. You're sick. You're fucking evil!"

She rose from her chair. "And worst of all, you've made me a hypocrite. I spend a lot of time preaching forgiveness to my patients, and I thought I had forgiven you. Now I don't know if I ever will. And you know the worst part?" Tears ran uncontrollably down her face. "It's that even through all this rage and hatred, I still love you. And now you'll die never having walked me down the aisle, never hugging me, and never saying the words back to me." Slumping, she fell back into the chair and rested her head on the bed. This time, she didn't stop the tears. She let her body shake, and she cried— cried for the little girl in her who'd never had a father, cried for the young adult whose father betrayed her, and she cried for the woman she was now.

For what felt like an eternity, Isla just laid there, half on the bed and half in her chair. She was physically and emotionally drained. Thankfully, no one came to interrupt or rush her, and for that, she was thankful.

Taking a deep breath, she slowly sat upright. She dried her eyes and checked her appearance in the mirror over the dresser then paused to focus on her reflection. "You can do this. It's the right thing to do. He would hate being dependent on others. The body lying in the bed is not him anymore, just the shell that used to hold him."

She turned and left the room to find Alex and the doctor.

5

She found them in the formal dining room area, combing through paperwork.

Alex took one look at her reddened nose and puffy eyes and jumped up to comfort her.

She waved him off. "No, please, you'll get me started again."

Alex nodded and stepped backward. "Say no more."

Isla gestured toward the papers. "What is all this?"

"Legalities. You'll need to sign stating you're agreeing to turn off the ventilator. And your father had documents drawn out stating his wishes for after his death."

She sat and listened as he explained each paper to her, and she wordlessly signed her name. So, Dad wanted to be cremated and buried next to her mother. That was shocking. Why couldn't he have just reached out to her? Things being said today didn't make sense when compared to the man she knew. He wanted a Catholic funeral? The man had never set foot inside a church, including the time he had her dropped off at the Abbey. He'd neither taken her himself nor picked her up.

She needed coffee. Hadn't Alex said something about a thermos full of coffee? Her vision blurred, and she couldn't see the paper.

"Isla, are we going too fast?" Alex asked, concerned.

She shook her head. "No, thank you. I was just remembering that you had coffee. I feel a headache coming on." She gently massaged her temples.

He surprised her by jumping up to retrieve it along with some aspirin. The man was a mystery; she didn't like mysteries.

"Thank you." She gratefully swallowed the pills and savored the hot liquid. Good Lord, it was exquisite. Had coffee ever tasted this good? He probably had it imported.

"Shall we continue?" the doctor asked.

"Yes please," she answered, feeling at least a little more human.

Once she had signed all the paperwork, they headed to her father's room. Daniel and Janice were already inside, waiting. Waiting for what? As she reached the threshold, she froze. What was she doing? This was a mistake. She could never go through with this, at least not today—maybe tomorrow. Yeah, tomorrow was a much better option. *No, stop! What are you doing? You're being a coward. You're just scared. You can do this.*

Without saying a word, Alex grabbed her hand and led her into the room.

"Now that we're all here, are there any questions?" the doctor addressed the room.

"How long will it take?" Isla asked.

"Because your father is on intravenous medication for low blood pressure and we are removing the life-sustaining measures, he will go pretty quickly. It could be minutes, or it could be hours, but he will pass today," he responded kindly.

"You told me he's not in pain. Will removing his machinery cause him to suffer? Will his last moments here be painful?"

"Who cares?" Daniel blurted. "Just get it over with!"

"No, I don't mind questions," the doctor assured. "It's important you know your loved one won't suffer. This is achieved by sedation and high doses of morphine."

"What do you mean, high doses? Will the morphine kill him?" *Oh God*, how can I do this? *Lord, please give me strength.*

"No, ma'am. By high dose, I mean ten to fifteen milligrams per hour. It is strictly comfort care."

"What will happen to his body? Will he start thrashing?" She saw Janice roll her eyes but chose to ignore her.

"Occasional muscle twitches and loss of reflexes in the legs and arms may occur, but please know this is involuntary. This is a process of dying, not your loved one coming back."

She nodded and, bracing herself for the next words, she clenched Alex's hand. "Okay, I trust you."

Upstairs in her father's room, the doctor checked the clock. "Please note the time is four thirty-eight p.m., and I am now stopping all life-sustaining machinery."

Isla watched as the doctor removed and powered off the ventilator. He disconnected medications for blood pressure, but the IV pump continued to push medications for pain and sedation. Her father's breathing was sporadic. She watched him go brief periods without breathing, each time wondering if it was the last, only for him to take several breaths in rapid succession.

This was brutal. The minutes dragged into hours. Daniel spouted curses about the time and left. Janice sniffed about being done with waiting on him and also left. Isla barely noticed. She was too focused on her father.

She put on soft music, the classical type he'd always preferred. She spoke to him, reliving the few positive memories she had with him.

Alex came and went from the room, wanting to check on her but also respecting the privacy of this time.

Though he never moved nor reacted in any way, Isla clung to the hope he could still hear her. She told him about her fears with marrying Alex. She told him about her achievements during the time she'd been away. She told him of her dreams for the future. She told him that while she had never wanted his money, she hoped she could use it to help the less fortunate.

When she felt she had said all there was to say, she had one last plea. "I'll be okay. It's okay to let go. Go be with my mother."

That seemed to be what he needed. Isla swore she watched him let go—a few more slow, shallow breaths and then none.

The next while was a blur—the doctor confirming his heart was no longer beating, the funeral home removing his body and assuring she could confirm arrangements tomorrow. The medical equipment company removed the machines. And then, nothing. The staff were gone, the doctor was gone, it was only Isla and Alex. Isla felt numb; the silence of the house made the chaos of her mind deafening.

*a*lex was torn between taking her in his arms and letting her cope in her own way. Finally, he gently stroked her cheek. "Come on, Isla, let me drive you to your hotel."

Desperation filled her face. Her voice was shaky as she asked, "Alex, will you take me to your place? I don't want to be alone tonight."

His breath caught in his chest at the idea of having her in his home among his belongings, the very place he craved her to be. He had to remind himself this wasn't a social visit; she needed him just as he'd always needed her. He couldn't and wouldn't screw this up. Words escaped him, so he proffered a beckoning hand.

Slowly she stood, wobbling.

He noticed the hour and realized she hadn't eaten but only a small sandwich all day.

Clasping his hand, she leaned into him and for a moment, and he didn't move,

God, he loved this woman. Ever so gently, he tilted her chin to his and lightly kissed her lips. It wasn't for lust or show but simply for comfort, for both of them. He scooped her into his arms and carried her to the car.

"Where are we going?" Isla asked as he pulled into town.

"Twenty-four-hour fast food, you need something in your stomach."

"Alex, there's no way I can eat right now."

"I know, that's why I'm ordering you a milkshake." He pulled in and rattled off his choices then paid and picked up the food. He passed her a peanut butter ice cream blend, and she took a sip. It could have been good, but it was wasted on her. She'd lost all sense of taste.

Finally, they reached their destination. She wasn't surprised to see his house was immaculate, a generous three-story brick mansion. Of course, it could fit into a corner of her father's house but so could the average Walmart. Still, by normal standards, it was massive. Old-fashion streetlights lit the paved circle driveway, and the landscape was beautifully manicured. A large lilac bush was the focal point inside the driveway enclosure. She loved lilacs; they had always been her scent and color.

The garage door opened, and Alex slid the car into its parking spot then came around to open her door. He lead her through a beautiful kitchen, one of her dreams with two sets of double stacks ovens. Alex had always been a great cook; it was one of the things she had in common with him and had drawn them together in the first place. Well, that and his looks certainly helped. They padded across perfectly glossed wood floors and up a soft carpeted stairway.

"You can use this room," he said, opening the door.

A beautiful four-post king-sized bed adorned in white and purple lace bed set was positioned between French doors leading to a patio and master bathroom where she could see a bathtub that looked heavenly. It was as if it had been designed especially for her.

"Feel free to use the shower. The bathroom is fully stocked with soaps and towels. I also recommend the jacuzzi. The jets are a good stress reliever, and you can choose from a variety of bath salts."

She smirked. "You use bath salts?"

He smiled back with furrowed eyes. "I have sisters. I'll see what I can find for you to put on. In the meantime, there are robes hanging in the closet. "

"Thank you."

"You're welcome." He wasn't ready to leave her, but he also couldn't afford to be selfish, so he shut the door and walked to his own room. His sisters and their families stayed here often, and he was sure one of the many outfits they had left would fit Isla, but he couldn't resist; he had to see her in nothing but one of his t-shirts again. From his dresser, he removed one of the tight white shirts he wore while exercising and smiled with satisfaction. With any luck, her hair would be wet and drip down … *Woah! Down, boy.* Still, he didn't change his mind for something more modest nor did he grab any sort of bottoms.

He needed to keep himself in check. Despite her telling Daniel they were getting married, he knew he still had to convince her. No reason he couldn't enjoy the view while he did so.

He knocked on the door to her room but got no response. He cracked the door. "Isla?" He heard the jets in the bathtub. The scent of exotic florals filled the room. He wavered. Did he place the t-shirt on the bed and go? Did he stick his head in to check on her? No, bad idea. He didn't trust himself not to touch her. Tonight was about her grief, and he couldn't afford to lose whatever shred of trust she was allowing him.

He laid his shirt on the bed for her and softly knocked on the bathroom door. "Isla, I've left a shirt on the bed for you. I'm sorry I didn't have anything more appropriate."

"Thank you, Alex," he heard her reply.

He hesitated, not wanting to leave. But her voice sounded steady and serene. He needed to give her some space right now.

7

*I*n the bathtub, Isla focused her energy on taking in the sensations of the moment. She blocked out all thoughts of the past and all worries about the future. There was only the now. The water was perfectly warm, relaxing her while the massaging jets soothed away the aches of the day. The bath oil she had found smelled of lilacs and vanilla with hints of lavender and roses. It made her imagine a tranquil garden, the kind she had always imagined where she would someday have to read and enjoy the summer heat.

She must have dozed off because the cold water was now draining on its own. Or ... was it?

"Don't worry. I'm not looking," Alex assured her when the water sloshed. "I don't want you catching a cold."

"Th-thank you." She shivered.

"Come here," he instructed gruffly, offering a thick, warm robe. His eyes were closed, so she slipped her arms in and snuggled the perfect fabric.

"This is nice." She stepped away from him. "Honestly, you've been wonderful today." She let her hair fall free from its tie. "But I don't understand you, Alex." Rotating the wedding ring on the finger, she turned to face him.

He put a finger to her lips and shushed her. "You're overthinking the situation. I want you to dry off, put on the shirt and lie down. You've been through a lot in the last two days, and you have more to come. You need to rest."

"Will you hold me? Just until I fall asleep?"

Alarms sounded in his brain, screaming, *Danger!* But he had to ignore them. Isla needed him, and he couldn't let her down. "You know I will." Alex turned down the bed blanket and gestured for her to climb in.

Isla appreciated the soft bed and fluffy pillows. She laid on her side, facing Alex.

Alex got in next to her and pulled the blanket over them. He slid one arm under her head and placed the other around her waist. He inhaled her scent as he nuzzled the top of her head. He soothingly stroked her back with the hand near her waist.

Isla appreciated the feeling of security she got lying in his powerful arms. Tomorrow, she would worry about protecting her mind and her heart. Tonight, she needed his presence to chase away the demons. Tonight, she needed him.

She must have been more tired than she thought; mercifully, dreams didn't haunt her—in fact, she might say it was the best night's sleep she'd had in years. Smilingly, she stretched and reached for Alex. A few more moments of make believe sounded just too tempting. But her hand met air. Springing upright, she opened her eyes and checked his side of the bed—empty. And just like that, the tears returned.

After a good ten-minute cry, she went to the bathroom and brushed her teeth. She couldn't even look at herself in the mirror; she was such a fool. A noise escaped her, and she quickly covered her mouth to hush it.

"Isla?" Alex asked from the other side of the door. Before she could respond or wipe her face, he entered, looking sexy as hell in low-cut sweatpants and nothing else.

"I'm fine," she answered automatically, raising her guard.

"I'm so sorry. I-I didn't want to wake you. I'd hoped to be back before you woke up." God, he felt like such a jackass.

"I said I'm fine," she repeated on her way past him. Then it was her turn to feel stupid. The smell of hot coffee and maple syrup hit her as she returned to the bedroom. "You made me breakfast?" She eyed the TV tray loaded with food beside the bed.

"I just know how full your day is today, and I remembered how much you love breakfast food."

She shook her head as she beheld the scene before her. Again, tears sprang from her eyes but for a completely different reason.

"I'm sorry, Isla. I'm going about this all wrong." He raked his hands over his hair in desperation.

"No." She turned to face him. "You're doing everything right." Slowly, she walked to him, every step taking a little more courage than the last. Slipping her arms around his neck, she went up on her tiptoes and kissed him, and he froze.

Before she could regret her boldness, he wrapped his arms around her and practically smashed her into him.

8

*A*ll reasonable thought left him, and he kissed her hard. He dug his fingers into her hips, and she gave as good as she got. She was turning him to liquid fire, and he lifted her off her feet and deposited them both onto the bed. He slid up her shirt to feel the smoothness of her abdomen.

She shivered under his touch and moaned in his mouth.

God, he couldn't get enough of her. Forcefully, he thrust his groin into hers—so much so that the bed shook, rattling the dishes. Pausing, he spied the TV tray. "Um … the food's getting cold."

"Are you really worried about food right now?" she asked on the verge of sexual frustration.

"That, and I-I don't have a condom in here." He looked her in the eye.

She smiled and reached for him. "Good, because I'm not on birth control."

It took him only a moment to register her words. His heart might have literally skipped a beat, then he resumed crushing her mouth with his. He frantically yanked off her shirt, and she pulled at his pants until she freed him of them.

Sweet Jesus, he was even more muscular than she remembered. Her hands couldn't get enough as they roamed over him. She wound her legs around his hips and arched into him.

"Goddammit, Isla, you're so fucking sexy." He examined her with hungry eyes then swooped down and took one of her breast into his hot, perfect mouth.

She cried out and thrust hard against him.

He released it and went to the other.

"Alex, please … Just fucking take me."

Releasing her swollen nipple, he gripped her thighs and looked at her before plunging in. He was completely inside her, and she shook from the pure bliss. They'd never been this close before, neither of them had wanted to risk pregnancy before, but now it was game on.

They made love like they'd never been apart, as if neither of them had forgotten the other's bodies or the things that sent them tumbling over the edge. And yet, it was hotter and needier than it'd ever been before.

They moved together, panted together, and exploded together. Isla swore she could see stars as she rode the wave of ecstasy and felt him fill her with his hot seed.

He couldn't breathe; he couldn't catch his fucking breath. With Isla pulsing beneath him, he didn't even want to leave her warmth. But, as they both came down from the high, he pulled out and kissed her. After rolling them to their sides, he cradled her head on his chest and intertwined their legs. He lazily ran his fingers over her back.

It was on the tip of his tongue to tell her he loved her, but he hesitated. She was going to marry him, and she was going to have his child. He'd been prepared to talk her into the idea, even offer separate houses and a surrogate all the while hoping for more. Now that he had her, he had everything. He just needed to make it official.

"Where did you get that ring?" he asked, running a finger over it.

"It was my mother's. It's been hidden for so long." She held it up to admire it. "It's nice to finally be able to show it off."

"It's stunning. Would you like one of your own? I had planned to buy you one."

She stilled at his question and brought her hand to his chest. "This one brings me hope and comfort. I think I'll enjoy seeing it on my finger. Anything else would feel cold and heavy."

His breath caught in his chest. *Cold and heavy? His ring would feel cold ... and heavy?* "Isla—"

"I need to ask you something, Alex." She hated to break the spell, but she had to know. "Were you actually going to cash that check my father wrote you ten years ago?"

"Yes, but—"

She shot up and reached for the disregard shirt. "Oh my god." What had she just done? Part of her had always longed and hoped it had all been a terrible misunderstanding.

"Isla, wait." He ripped the shirt from her hands, and she slapped him hard across the face—once, then twice—as she cried out in shame and utter agony. "Goddammit, woman!" He gripped her wrists and pinned her to him. "Let me explain."

She shook her head, and it only infuriated him more.

"Yes," he commanded firmly. "You wouldn't listen then, but before you leave this bed, you *will* hear my side of story."

Surrendering, she nodded. When he loosened his hold, she reached for the sheet to cover herself and scooted away from him, but she didn't leave.

41

"Your father approached my father about the idea of marriage. He wanted you with someone successful, and he knew I was enrolled in law school and that I came from a respectable and wealthy family. He also wanted someone strong willed enough who could handle you."

She wiped away a tear but said nothing.

"Isla, I never meant to fall in love with you. I didn't even want to meet you. I mean, what kind of man has to sell his daughter? For ten million dollars no less. I went to your house out of respect for my own father, fully prepared to politely refuse the offer. But then I saw you standing in the kitchen with flour on your face and your hands in dough. You were nothing like I had expected. I thought you must be a terrible, spoiled princess, but, in that moment, all I saw was genuine. I decided to get to know you, and after I did, the idea of marriage was exactly what I wanted with you."

"Then why take the money?"

"Because I knew how controlling your father was. He'd have never let me marry you if he knew I supported your dreams."

"I was twenty years old, Alex. He didn't have a say in who I married."

"I know you think that, but I wanted his blessing. I wanted to get you out of that house. Don't you see, Isla? I wanted to save you. "

"But you settled for destruction instead. Did you have to play the part so well? Why didn't you just tell me from the beginning instead of letting Daniel blindside me with it?"

"Hindsight's twenty/twenty, darling. Obviously, now I realize I should have told you. I had convinced myself it didn't matter what had brought us together. And I promise you I had no idea your brother knew, let alone that he would use it to hurt you. Or that it would take ten years to find you again."

"I didn't want to be found, Alex. You hurt me worse than my family ever had. It took a long time to heal."

"Would it help to know your father hired a couple of thugs to beat the hell out of me when he found out I deflowered you before marriage?"

"Only if it were true," she said with a half-smile.

"Believe me, it's true. You wanna talk about taking a long time to heal? I took your virtue, and you left. He was convinced you'd come back ruined."

"I guess he was right, because I did." She pulled her knees into her chest. "Oh god, Alex, what are we doing? We can't have a baby. Oh god." She sprang from the bed. "I gotta find a way to flush this out of me." She darted toward the bathroom but not quickly enough.

"Isla, what are you doing?" Alex asked, stopping her.

"I can't, in good conscience, pass my genes to an innocent baby. Mental illness, depression, anxiety—all that crap is hereditary."

"Yes, but our baby won't have any of that. He or she will be raised in a healthy, loving environment."

"Oh god, what if I can't give birth? What if I die just like my mother did and you're left with an eternal reminder just like my father?"

"Isla, slow down. Breathe." He escorted her to the bed. "None of that will happen. Technology has come a long way since then. We'll hire the best doctors to monitor you both every step of the way. We'll plan a c-section if we have to. We will get through this." He handed her his shirt then pulled on his pants. "Let me reheat the food. You'll feel better on a full stomach."

Isla watched Alex gather the food and leave the room.

She hurried into the bathroom for a quick shower. Despite Alex's reassurances, doubts plagued her. How could she have been so reckless and impulsive? She was nowhere near ready to have a child.

She cranked the water to punishingly hot, as if it could somehow erase her actions from the past hour. She scrubbed her body and dried off. Then she remembered she had no clean clothes. She sighed. She would have to have Alex bring her to her hotel room before she went to the funeral home.

9

The days were a blur as the funeral approached. Isla remained at the hotel, insisting she needed to clear her mind for what was coming. She spoke to distant relatives. She spoke to her father's business associates. She answered question after question and felt like she was on repeat, telling the same story over and over. Everyone wanted to know how the larger-than-life Robert Goldwen had met such an abrupt end.

Finally, the day of the funeral arrived. Isla dressed in a sensible long-sleeve, knee-length black dress with scoop neckline she had purchased. She wore black flats and a small pair of diamond studs. Her long auburn-colored hair flowed freely around her face and shoulders. She studied her reflection in the mirror and decided she looked appropriate for the occasion.

Alex had offered to drive her, but she wanted to know she could make a quick exit if Daniel or Janice got to be too much. She also was trying desperately to maintain some distance between her and Alex after her terrible lapse in judgment. She was glad Alex was not pushing the matter. She didn't think she could fight herself and him too.

At the church, Isla sat in the front row and ensured to sit next to her father's cousins who had come, so as to avoid being seated next to Daniel or Janice. Alex sat beside her, dutifully playing the role of devoted fiancé. To Isla's surprise, the large church was filled. Countless people came to pay their respects to the man who was outwardly a pillar of the community. He had employed people at a variety of businesses he had owned. He had donated the money to build a new and improved maternity ward and NICU at the local hospital. While Isla did not recall her father being close to anyone, he had certainly made an impact on the town. She wondered how many people would have come if they had seen him the way she did.

The priest began the service. Isla listened closely to the words about God's promise for the afterlife. She wondered if her father had found Jesus during her absence and if that was why he'd chosen the service he had. Finally, the service ended. The funeral director loaded the urn with her father's ashes into the hearse. The funeral procession went to the cemetery. They asked Isla to place the urn into the place next to where her mother lay. The priest spoke some more. He acknowledged her and Daniel and Janice, asking each to throw a shovel of dirt into the grave. Finally, it was over. People trickled out of the cemetery. Many came to talk to Isla, expressing condolences and their desire to catch up now that she was back in town.

Isla carefully kept busy, ensuring she was not alone to be cornered by Alex, Daniel, or Janice. Finally, she could not avoid them any longer. She saw Daniel approaching her, and she bolted to Alex's side. He was definitely a safer option than Daniel.

Surprised, Alex brought an arm around her shoulders. His ego deflated a little when he saw Daniel approaching and realized he was just her escape goat.

"A wonderful service, don't you think, Daniel?" Alex asked before he could utter the first word.

"Yeah yeah, very moving and blah blah. I didn't come to talk about that. When are you doing the official reading of the will? I want my sister's things out of my house. That'll be Mother's room from now on."

"Let's head there now. Oh, and Daniel, I wouldn't get cocky just yet."

WHEN EVERYONE WAS SEATED in the formal dining room, Alex produced a copy of the official will and last testimony of Robert Goldwen. Once again, he recited the terms for which each of Robert's children had to obey to collect their inheritance and, of course, the consequences of disobedience.

Anna jumped up, finally understanding why her presence had been requested. "Oh, hell no! If you think I'll marry that arrogant drunk and let him touch me long enough to impregnate me, you are out of your damn mind!"

"Oh, come off it, Anna," Daniel barked. "It's only five years, and you'll be well compensated."

"There isn't enough money in the world to make me choose such a disgusting proposal."

"Is that so? I seem to remember a time you were begging me to put a ring on it."

"That was before I found out I was part of your long list of conquests and bragging rights to your friends. Something is seriously wrong with you, Daniel, and, if you even think about pursuing this, you'll end up in the manure pit again. Only this time, you might not make it out."

"Anna darling, don't be hasty," Janice interjected smoothly. "Your family's farm is in danger of going under. Think of them. If you won't do it for yourself, do it for them."

"Are you really trying to use emotional blackmail on me? Do yourself a favor and invest in a good therapist, because ya'll are crazy as fuck if you think your money for my happiness is something my family would ever be okay with. Save yourself some money and get a family counselor you can see together. No offense, Isla."

Isla held up her hands and grinned. "None taken. I actually happen to know several good shrinks, although I'm not sure if any of them would be up for such a hopeless challenge."

"Yes, of course you would know several, dear," Janice agreed. "I imagine it'll take a whole crew of them to fix you."

"I'm out of here. And, Daniel, stay the hell away from me. My daddy's got a gun and several animals hanging on the wall. He doesn't need to add a human."

Daniel rose as if to follow her out, but Alex put a hand on his shoulder and pushed him into his seat.

"As for the matter of the house, it belongs to neither of you until one or both of you complete your duties. At that time, you can opt to sell it and split the money or buy out the other person. Meanwhile, neither of you may live here. It will, however, maintain its staff and upkeep until permanent ownership is granted."

Daniel violently slammed his fists on the table. "This is bullshit! She left! She doesn't even live here, and she's just half-blood!"

"I don't make the rules, Daniel. I just read them off. Isla has just as much of your father's DNA as you do. You are equal heirs and regarded as such," Alex coolly pointed out.

Janice rose. "Let's go, Daniel. We need to reconvene. This isn't over yet."

"I'm not finished yet," Alex stated. "There's still the matter of his other properties."

"Robert knew his will would cause a feud between the three of you. He also knew Daniel would assume he would continue to live here. Daniel, your father purchased a modest house outside the city limits for you. It has just one bedroom, as he wants you to separate from your mother's apron strings. It has been updated and is to remain yours whether you inherit the money. He's also paying for an extended stay in a rehabilitation facility of Isla's choosing. Due to her education and career choice, he believed she would be the family member with the best knowledge and experience to make such an important decision."

Before Daniel exploded, his mother placed a reassuring hand on his shoulder. "Don't worry, Daniel. That part is optional. We'll discuss it more later. There's no way I'm trusting that flea with you."

"Janice, Robert left you an apartment in Manhattan. Fully furnished, with a view. He wanted you far away from Isla and Daniel, and he felt the best way to do that was to ensure you were living somewhere that would appeal to your ego more than trying to fix Daniel's possible marriage to Anna."

"Isla, you are to inherit your grandparents' cabin in Wyoming, as well as a small house here in town. Robert wanted you to reconnect with me and the community, but he also knew how much you loved the mountain cabin on the lake."

Despite Daniel's and Janice's whining about the

unfairness of it all, Isla's heart sang. She had no idea what house she would have here in town, but she was glad she would not have to choose between living at the hotel or moving straight in with Alex. And her grandparents' cabin was the place she had considered her sanctuary as a child. Daniel had hated it, so Isla had spent many summers there with the grandparents who'd adored her. She had caught frogs, swam in the lake, chased butterflies, and laid on her back, stargazing. It was the one place she could just be a kid. The thought of returning there again filled her heart with joy.

Alex continued to read. Her father had left various holdings to local charities. He had created trust funds to ensure comfortable retirement to his most trusted longtime staff. The list went on. Isla wondered at the extensive assets, imagining what her life would have been like had he been one tenth as devoted to fatherhood as he was to business.

At long last, Alex was done reading.

Daniel stormed off to his room.

Janice appeared pleased with the idea of Manhattan and hurried off to pack.

Again, Isla found herself alone with Alex. "Have you seen the house he left me?"

"I have not. I have the address here, but I have never been there."

"Fair enough. I will check it out tomorrow. Tonight, I just want sleep."

"Can I give you a lift?"

She shook her head. "Not yet. I want to get one more thing from my old room."

Though he wasn't invited, he followed her up and into her closet where she rummaged through multiple garment bags, zipping and unzipping them. "What are you looking for?"

"The dress I wore to the black and white ball for the

children's cancer society benefit in oh-nine. I figure it can serve as a wedding dress now, provided it still fits."

"But I've already seen you in that dress, Isla," Alex pointed out as she had her *ah-ha* moment.

She shrugged and inspected the lace. "I'm not superstitious."

"Well, maybe I am. Honestly, Isla, I'd prefer it if you bought a new dress."

She closed the bag and faced him. "Truthfully, Alex, I can't afford it. I still have to go home, pack my things, pay to break the lease on my apartment, quit my job and find a new one here. I can't afford another dress, and I don't need to when this one is perfectly fine."

"But I can, Isla." He removed a black credit card and offered it to her. "You don't want me to buy you a new ring, but please let me buy you a proper wedding dress."

She hesitated. "I can't take your money, Alex."

"We'll be married soon." Stepping forward, he slipped the card into her back pocket.

The slight contact made her shiver.

"What's mine is yours now. And, Isla ..." He leaned in close to whisper in her ear.

Another shiver raked her body as his breath hit her neck in just the right way.

"Buy yourself a sweater while you're at it. I noticed you seem to get cold easily."

"Fuck you," she growled a little too breathlessly.

"Gladly." He stole a brief kiss before she could protest. "As for the other matters you mentioned, I'll hire a moving company to pack and ship your belongings to the new house. I'll work out a deal with your landlord and email your boss, explaining the situation. Not to mention I have plenty of money, you'll only need to work if you want to."

51

"Jesus, Alex, you can't just step in and take over my life." She pushed him away. "I actually have friends there I'd like to say goodbye to."

"Great! I'd love to meet your friends. Invite them to the wedding."

"We're not having that kind of wedding. We're going to the courthouse or Vegas or wherever people go to these days for a quick *I do*."

"I don't think so, darling. I plan to show you off to the world. I already have a wedding planner on retainer. We just need to give her a date."

"You have a wedding planner? You don't even know what kind of flowers I like."

"Lilacs."

"Okay, but you don't know my favorite color."

"Violet."

"Well ... you don't know everything!"

"I know you prefer chicken over beef, your favorite cake is red velvet, and you love candlelit. You like nice, sweet wine, and you enjoy dancing. Isla, I know you, and what I don't know I'll learn over time," he told her gently. He was dealing with a caged animal, and he couldn't let her escape.

"Fine. So whatever you want! Just tell me when and where. I have more important things to worry about."

"Isla ..." He reached for her as she went to storm past him.

"No. I buried my father today. I'm not ready for another funeral—oh sorry, *wedding*." She needed to get out of here. In her haste, she ran from the bedroom and straight into Daniel.

10

"Trouble in paradise, sis?" he asked with booze-coated breath.

"Why don't you worry about your damn self?"

"Oh, I don't have to. You'll never make it. I know you're staying at the hotel. If you had any common sense, you'd lie on your back for the next five years and take a pounding like every other good wife."

She saw red, something snapped inside her, and she flew at him, only to find herself in the iron clasp of Alex's arm. Bucking wildly, she kicked in her brother's direction.

"Walk away, Daniel," Alex warned.

Smiling, he headed for the stairs.

"Where are you going?" Isla screamed, still trying to break free.

"Gas station. I'm out of beer." He smiled wickedly.

"Are you insane? A drunk driver killed our father!"

"I had nothing to do with that!" Daniel hit the hallway table and knocked its contents on the floor. He stormed from the house and tore out of the driveway as if someone was chasing him.

Alex cursed that he couldn't stop Daniel from leaving. The damn fool would wind up killing himself or someone else, or both. But he had to focus on keeping Isla from starting a physical confrontation, and so Daniel left.

"We need to stop him, Alex." The anxiety was high in her voice. "We can't let him drive in that condition. He's a danger to everyone on the road!"

"You're right. I'll call the sheriff's department and report him. Hopefully, they find him before anyone gets hurt."

DANIEL DROVE his expensive sports car the way it was meant to be driven—fast. In his drunken state, he was unaware that he was weaving. He took the curve faster than he should have, only to encounter several deer standing in the road. Daniel swerved to avoid them then lost control and crashed into a tree.

The next thing Daniel knew, he was on a stretcher, surrounded by flashing lights, and loaded into the ambulance. He could see his car, smashed into a large oak tree. The ambulance doors closed, and the siren activated on as they sped toward the hospital.

In the emergency room, nurses poked and prodded Daniel. They drew blood and ran tests. He cursed the doctors for not letting him go home, though they told him they had to run tests due to the loss of consciousness. At last, the doctor confirmed he had no serious injuries, just a concussion and a gash on his forehead from hitting the steering wheel.

"So, I can go home now?"

The doctor seemed nervous and stated he would write the discharge order.

After the doctor left, two uniformed police officers entered the hospital room.

"What do you want?" he snarled.

"Mr. Goldwen, I'm afraid you're going to have to come with us. Get dressed."

"I'm not going anywhere with you. I haven't done anything wrong!"

"Your sister called us when you left earlier tonight, stating you had been drinking prior to leaving."

"That meddling busybody is exaggerating. I had two beers. Nothing to get worked up about. She's just trying to cause problems for me."

"Mr. Goldwen, your bloodwork shows your blood alcohol content was more than three times the legal limit. And the stretch of road you were on is rather remote. I would say if your sister hadn't called and told us where you were going, you likely would still be trapped in the car. No one would have seen you for hours. Now get dressed."

"Can I at least get a moment of privacy?"

"You can go to the bathroom. We will be waiting when you get done."

After he was dressed, the officers handcuffed Daniel and walked him through the hospital to the police car like a common criminal. He was enraged; he felt violated, and he was sure somehow these officers had trampled on his rights. He took comfort knowing his mother knew many local police officers due to her charity work. She would have someone's head for the embarrassment of arresting her son.

"I want my phone call!" Daniel hollered when they entered the police station.

Though the officers on duty didn't appreciate the attitude, they also knew his father had just passed away, and it was right.

Seated at a desk, he punched in his mother's number only to be sent straight to voicemail. He cursed angrily under his breath. Gripping the receiver, he was tempted to crush it with his bare hands, but that wouldn't solve his problem, and he couldn't stay here. Swallowing a bit of his pride, he called Isla who answered on the first ring.

"Isla, I need a ride," he said gruffly.

"Oh, thank god, you scared me to death, asshole. I saw your car. Where are you? Are you okay?"

"I'm at the police station. I need you to bail me out." Saying the words damn near killed him, and he was met with silence. "Isla, ya there?"

"I'm here."

"Please, you gotta get me out of here. I can't stay in these small quarters. You know I'm claustrophobic."

"I know. But I can't get you, Daniel. You need help. You need to be held accountable."

"Isla, don't do this to me!"

"I didn't. You've done this to yourself. I'm sorry."

When he heard Isla hang up the phone, he felt completely helpless for the first time in his life. He didn't have his father's money or his mother's persuasion to bail him out. So, he switched gears and channeled his anger. Anger was safer; he couldn't be seen as vulnerable.

IN HER HOTEL ROOM, Isla fretted. Had she done the right thing? The sister in her felt justified in making him face the consequences of his actions, that he would never learn if he was constantly enabled. The therapist in her knew he must have found it incredibly difficult to have to ask her of all people for help. And she worried about the absolute hell he must be in due to his claustrophobia. Another scar that could be attributed to Janice, she thought bitterly, remembering how Janice would lock them in small dark closets far away from the main part of the house where she couldn't hear their cries, begging to be let out, screaming apologies for whatever minor infractions she had been so angered by.

The guilt became overwhelming. She wanted Daniel to learn he couldn't just do whatever he wanted. But knowing the horrors they had both faced at the hands of his mother, she wavered. She knew addiction was often a coping mechanism to deal with trauma. Could she really expect him to cope better with his past by putting him through further trauma that would reopen old wounds?

Sighing heavily, she gave up on sleep and got dressed. Daniel might be a lost cause, but she couldn't ignore the desperate tone she had heard in his voice. She couldn't be responsible for damaging him further. She grabbed her keys and headed to the jail.

At the jail, Isla signed the appropriate paperwork and handed over the money she had pulled from the ATM.

"Goldwen, ya made bail!" the guard hollered as they approached.

Isla watched first the look of relief cross his face and then surprise.

He didn't speak as the guard unlocked the cell and led him to the exit. What could he say? He'd been awful to her and still she came. His own mother couldn't be bothered now that she had a little of his father's money again.

Isla didn't talk either, just led him to his car. Once inside, she handed him a bottle of water and a few pills. "I picked up your prescriptions."

He swallowed without questioning her.

She slowly drove them to her father's house. She called Alex, who was now on her speed dial.

Even though it was after midnight, he answered on the third ring. "Isla?" he asked groggily. "You okay?"

"I'm okay." She hesitated before asking for a favor. If Daniel could reach out to her, she'd take a page from his book and ask Alex for help. "Can you meet me at my father's please?"

"Hmm?" he mumbled sleepily. "Just come here, Isla. I'll give you the code.

Again, she paused. "I have Daniel. And I was hoping you would stay the night with us." Her anxiety was on high alert, and her throat felt like it was tightening.

"You have Daniel?" he asked, sounding awake for the first time. "I thought you were going to practice tough love?"

"I did ... for about three hours."

"Isla, when we have children, I'm doing the disciplining. I'll be there soon."

Relief engulfed her and ... was it warmth? Absentmindedly, she touched her stomach. *When we have children,* she repeated—plural—more than was required. The idea wasn't terrible, but how would they do co-parenting?

DANIEL WAS ANNOYED; he didn't need a male babysitter—hell, he didn't need a babysitter period. Least of all Alex the prick. What he needed was a beer. Remembering he was out made him grit his teeth. There was no way Isla would buy him any, and he'd already asked her for more than he'd ever wanted to. Why had she picked him up?

For perhaps the first time in a long time, Daniel felt sorry for her. Their father really was an asshole. How could he force such a man on his sister? A gold digging, career-minded, self-centered prick. At least Anna was soft hearted and kind. *Anna,* he thought. He'd royally screwed up with her. She thought she could save him, but he was never good enough for her. No matter how he messed up, she never lost faith in him. His mother hadn't liked her; she'd been nasty, so he'd done the only thing he could to protect her. He destroyed her; it was the only real way to keep her safe.

He eyed his sister. He'd destroyed her as well. When he learned the truth about Alex, he had blurted it out in the cruelest way possible. She wouldn't have listened to kindness, and he couldn't let her end up with him. They'd both suffered enough from people who should love them but didn't. It was no life.

He'd never dreamed it would send her packing. In his mind, it was her biggest offense. How could she have left him alone in that house? His mother was even crueler to him, with her out of the picture to take the blunt of. That was the year he got his driver's license and first fake ID. He wasn't an alcoholic; he could quit any time he wanted to. But why would he quit something he loved? You wouldn't ask a baseball player to quit hitting balls; it was the same thing.

Oh, Alex was not happy. What in the hell had she been thinking? Now he was the one driving too fast. The woman's heart amazed him, but a good heart had never protected her from Daniel before, and he sure as hell didn't think it would now. The bastard couldn't be trusted, not with her. She might be Daniel's blood, but she was *his* family now.

59

11

He reached the house and was surprised to find the two of them sitting at the table, sipping hot chocolate. The tension was still present but was civilized. They hadn't noticed his entry, so he held back and listened.

Isla's voice sounded serious. "I know we've both had it rough. But you can't let it ruin the rest of your life."

Daniel's voice sounded tired and pained. "I don't know how else to block it out. Everything triggers memories. So many places in this house remind me of being yelled at, ridiculed, shamed, or locked in the godforsaken closet."

Isla softly murmured, "Perhaps a change of scenery will help. Maybe the new house is a blessing in disguise."

Daniel rolled his eyes. "Of course, you would say that. You choose to live like a pauper."

Isla ignored the barb. "Think about it. The new house won't have those memories. And with Father gone and Janice several states away, you won't have those reminders either. Nor the constant nagging about what you should be doing, the put downs for simply being within eyesight."

Daniel scowled. "Right. Because the best way to get over it is living in poverty."

Alex decided to reveal himself. He pretended he hadn't been eavesdropping. "Daniel, good to see you are in one piece."

"Sure ya are. I'm going to bed," he said to Isla before walking away.

Alex raised an eyebrow at Isla. "Care to explain yourself?"

She blew out a breath and avoided eye contact. "No."

"Dammit, Isla, you should have called me with your decision. I don't want you alone with him, especially in a car."

"The man has a concussion, Alex. Between that and his emotional state, he wasn't a threat. Before you say anything, stop. There's actually a lot you don't know. Things I've never told you, things I've never even revealed in counseling because I can't. It's not just painful, it's embarrassing, and I can't deal with the shame. He's an ass, okay? We agree, but he's the only one who knows and remains haunted by the same memories. I'm going to stop swiping at him and start acting like a sister."

Alex silently relaxed his hands at his sides, not knowing what to say.

"I need to research rehabilitation centers. He can't be dropped off just anywhere. This isn't just about alcohol." She looked at him with desperation. "I've been so consumed with jealousy and hate ..." Tears fell, and Alex dropped to his knees in front of her chair.

He held her face in his hands. "Okay." He pulled her into him and let her cry.

61

As Isla lay asleep in his arms, he was plagued with guilt. How had he never pressed for more information about the rivalry between the siblings? He knew it wasn't normal, but he just assumed it must be a half-blood thing. After all, he couldn't imagine life without his two sisters. Not to mention he had his own reasons for hating Daniel; he'd been the one to spill the beans and send her running. Now he needed to let go of the past and focus on the present.

Presently, as much as he was enjoying Isla laying asleep on him, his back was screaming to get off the fancy couch that was more for looks than comfort. He gently stroked his thumb across her cheek and murmured her name.

Isla stirred but did not open her eyes.

His heart melted at the sight. God, how he had missed little moments such as this. Carefully, he scooped her in his arms and carried her toward her old bedroom. He knew no one would care if the siblings stayed one last night in the family home.

Alex tenderly placed Isla in her bed and covered her. He watched her sleep, yearning to join her. Sighing, he tiptoed out and checked on Daniel. At last, he turned and found a room nearby to sleep in. He left the door open to ensure he could hear if any disagreements arose.

Isla wasn't sure she'd slept more than a few hours. By 5 a.m., she was sitting in her father's old office, searching the web. Several cups of coffee later and she had found the perfect place. A high-end spa with an indoor pool, basketball courts, and gourmet meals. The rooms were less hospital and more hotel. The counselors had amazing reviews, and many of them were recovering from their own problems, making them relatable. If she had to send him away for several months, at least it was to a place nearly as big as their father's house sitting on one hundred acres. She just hoped he didn't fight it.

She needed a mental break. After shutting down the computer, she headed to the kitchen. She owed Alex breakfast, and cooking always relaxed her. With the music on low, she hummed while she baked cinnamon rolls and flipped bacon. The table was already set with crepes, biscuits and gravy, eggs, and sausage links. She may have gone a little overboard, but hey, she was having too much fun to quit.

Alex leaned against the doorjamb to the kitchen as déjà vu hit him.

Isla was dancing around the kitchen with flour on her face and in her hair. She made quite a sight for sore eyes.

"Smells great," he said while, simultaneously, Daniel said, "Jesus, why are you awake?"

Isla startled at the voices with a hand to her heart and shut off the radio. "Oh, good, you're both awake. I made breakfast."

Again, they spoke at the same time. "Thanks," Alex said while Daniel said, "For who? The whole damn household?"

She shrugged. "Sure. Why shouldn't they eat. Breakfast is the most important meal of the day."

Daniel grunted and stuck a few pieces of bacon into his mouth. "This orange juice needs vodka."

Isla ignored him. "Everything is ready. Let's eat. I don't know about you, but I could use some coffee and food before I see the house our father chose for me. What are your plans, Daniel?"

Daniel scowled. "Living the good life in my new one-bedroom shack." He crammed a giant bite of cinnamon roll into his mouth. He didn't want to tell Isla he was already craving a drink. She would start acting like a shrink again and suggest he was addicted. He just needed something to take off the edge. Didn't he deserve that after his father's death and subsequent betrayal?

Isla frowned at the dark expression on her brother's face. She knew the idea of a small house was a blow to his ego, but she believed it would do him a world of good to be free of the memories haunting their father's house. "Would you like me to come with you to check it out?"

"I'm a big boy, sis. I think I can manage to put the address in my GPS and drive there on my own. You don't need to hold my hand."

Isla shook her head at his bitterness. "Your car isn't driveable."

"Then I guess I'll use our driver," he said as if saying *duh*.

"I'd like you to take a look at something else." She slid the papers she'd printed across the table.

Daniel barely glanced at them before pounding his fist on the table. "Goddammit, I don't need to go to some kumbaya center for sniveling weaklings with no self-control! There's nothing wrong with having a couple drinks!"

Alex couldn't hold his tongue any longer. "You selfish, arrogant prick! You could have died last night or killed someone else! My god, are you really so far gone that you think you're above the laws of nature and man?"

"I swerved to miss a group of deer! It had nothing to do with the alcohol, you stupid bastard."

"The police told Isla your blood alcohol was three times the legal limit. And no skid marks were on the road, meaning you didn't even slam on the brakes. Don't you think one funeral is enough for one week?"

Daniel shoved his chair backward and stood. "Screw you both. I'm out of here." He stormed out of the house.

*I*sla busied herself organizing the papers.

"Isla," Alex said, stilling her hands. "Spend the day with me today. Let me spoil you and relieve some of the stress."

"I don't know, Alex." She pulled away. "I need to go to the house, and I gotta figure out how to get Daniel to this rehab center."

"We'll look at the house, make some phone calls to figure out availability, and then I'm whisking you away. And I'm not taking no for an answer."

Isla really didn't want to deny him; he made a compelling case, not to mention it had been a long time since she'd been spoiled. Blowing a stray hair out of her face, she said, "Fine," feigning indifference. "I need to shower first. And clean this mess."

"I can take care of the food. Unless you'd rather I help you with your shower?" he asked with a wink.

"I'll manage," she said dryly. She turned away before he could see the heat in her cheeks and headed upstairs.

She found a collection of soaps in the hallway closet.

Some things never change. Using the shower adjacent to her old room, she cranked the heat and sighed. God, her life was a mess. She'd love nothing more than to forget her obligations and stay in this shower for the rest of the day. Giving in, she got out and towel dried. She rummaged through her old dresser and removed a pair of jeans and a long-sleeve shirt. Straining to get the pants over her butt and zipped, she concluded she was no longer the same size. But, hey, if they zip, they fit; it's woman's logic. And yeah, the shirt was like a second skin, but she only had to wear it long enough to get to the hotel. After today, she'd have a house and, soon, the rest of her belongings and wouldn't have to be in this situation again.

Walking was a little difficult, so she did a few squats to try and stretch the jeans before she headed down.

Alex rose when he caught sight of Isla, cutting off the person on the other line of his phone. "I don't care what it costs, make it happen. Yes!" he barked. "Good, we'll see you tomorrow." Then, without saying goodbye, he hung up.

She twisted her fingers together. "Who was that?"

"The beach house rehab center. They have an opening tomorrow."

"Guess we just need to figure out how to get him there."

"I've already thought about that. I'll have the driver stock the limo with his favorite booze and tell him they're going to the casino. He'll be too lit to argue when they get there."

"You're suggesting we lie to him?"

"You have a better plan?"

"I guess not. It's actually pretty brilliant, and he'll get one last hurrah."

"ISLA," he asked, following her to the car. "Are you trying to kill me?"

"What?" Confused, she turned to face him.

"Those jeans fit you a little too well."

"They're a little tight is all."

"Well, now my pants are a little too tight."

She bit her lower lip and felt herself blush. Butterflies danced in her stomach as she remembered just how amazing that part of him felt inside her. Before she could comprehend what was happening, Alex had pinned her between himself and the passenger side of the car.

"You'll be the death of me, woman," he said roughly before swooping in and stealing her lips with his own.

She moaned as his hands traveled from her waist, past her hips, and landed on her butt.

He squeezed her, bringing their groins flush with each other, causing her to whimper. His mouth left hers to find the sensitive spot on her neck, and she gripped his hair. He lifted her slightly, and she wrapped her legs around his waist.

"Alex," she whispered as his lips met hers once again.

He responded by rocking into her and feeling his way up her shirt until his hand found her taut nipple.

She gasped at the contact and bucked against him.

"I want you, Isla," he told her, showing no signs of restraint. "I want to take you right now against this car."

She was about to agree, but he straightened her shirt and placed her on her feet.

Yanking open the door, he practically shoved her onto the seat. "But too many people here are coming and going, and I don't want them seeing parts of you that only belong to me." He slammed the door harder than necessary and strode to the driver's side. He clenched the steering wheel, and neither of them spoke as he drove to her new house.

It was only a five-minute drive from his home but still too far in his opinion. He didn't want her living anywhere that wasn't with him. Fortunately, the wedding was right around the corner, and he planned to have living arrangements agreed upon by then.

Isla was happily surprised by the house her father had left her. It was a white two-story house with black shutters and a wraparound porch. The front and back yards were spacious. A porch swing hung in the back across from a tree that looked perfect for a future treehouse. Inside were four bedrooms, a first-floor office with a view of the garden, and a well-equipped kitchen. The master suite was tastefully decorated, with a king-sized bed covered with a luxurious-looking ruched comforter. The master bathroom had a spacious shower and a large garden tub. Indeed, the house was simple but perfect for Isla. It felt like a family home. Isla could easily picture sipping lemonade on the porch swing while watching her children play tag in the back yard.

Alex could see from Isla's face as she went room to room that she was pleased. He was disappointed. He had secretly hoped she would hate it, making it easier for him to persuade her to move in with him. However, the dreamy smile on her face warmed him. It was good to see her looking so blissfully hopeful. In this moment, she was not worrying about Daniel, the will, or their wedding. She was simply enjoying the moment and anticipating the future.

"Well, this is a surprise," Isla said as they gave the house one last glance on the way to the hotel so she could check out and drop off her things at home. *Home. Wow, maybe life here wouldn't be so bad after all.*

"Indeed," was all he said.

Alex waited patiently as Isla grabbed her things and paid the bill. Afterward he dropped her off to her car and promised to swing by the new place soon.

"No rush," she said, deflating his ego a little. "I need to run to the store to get the essentials. Toilet paper, shampoo, groceries," she rattled off. He nodded and then left her, he too had some shopping to do.

Isla walked down every aisle in the market. Her hand hovered as she reached for a box of tampons. Would she need them? Well, she wouldn't know for a couple more weeks but still, better safe than sorry. She dropped the box in along with condoms—not that she was planning on using them, but they'd already been together once, and today was almost a second time.

At her place, she put away things and set a fresh vase of flowers on the dining room table. She'd have to find a place to donate her old furniture to. There was no sense in shipping it here when the house was already so beautifully furnished.

Sinking into the soft bed in the master room, she closed her eyes and moaned in contentment. She'd just take a moment to rest, then she'd start lunch preparations.

Alex arrived to find her asleep and chose not to wake her. He knew sleep hadn't been coming easily to her and didn't want to interrupt. Instead, he busied himself contacting the movers who would be handling Isla's apartment.

When he heard Isla waking, he traipsed to the kitchen and checked the soup he'd started. It smelled amazing, and he had fresh baked bread to go with it. He set the table and poured them each a glass of water. If things progressed the way he hoped, he wanted them both to be sober.

ISLA AWOKE to the aroma of food, and her stomach growled in anticipation. *Alex* ... She checked her phone and couldn't believe she had been sleeping for over two hours. She slid off the side of the bed and felt the plush carpet between her bare toes. She yawned and sauntered downstairs to the kitchen.

Alex had made broccoli cheese soup and crusty French bread. Alex served her, and she eagerly enjoyed both. Damn, the man could cook.

Alex was glad to see Isla eating with such fervor. She was too quick to skip meals when she was stressed. He cleared his throat. "Isla, have you given any more thought to what you want for our wedding?"

"Not really. It would be different if we were getting married for the right reasons, if we were madly in love and planning to stay together. But we're not that couple. Even if we manage to stay together for the five years, we are not a love match. If you want a lot of fanfare and hoopla, I won't stop you. I just don't see the point."

Her words cut him like a knife to the chest. He knew Isla wasn't marrying him for love, but to hear say it so bluntly was brutal. "I told you I love you. I don't give a damn about your father's money. I've made my own fortune. I want you as my wife, not for five years but forever. And I want our wedding to be a day we tell our children about, a day they dream of recreating when they imagine their weddings."

Isla wanted desperately to believe him, but she couldn't let down her guard. She shrugged. "Suit yourself. I would rather plan the honeymoon trip."

Alex grinned naughtily. "Oh, do tell."

Isla punched him in the arm. "I mean, where we'll go, where we'll stay, and things to do. *Outside* the bedroom," she specified at his wiggling eyebrows. "I haven't been on a proper vacation in years. I want to go somewhere warm and tropical. I want to go hiking, experience the local cuisine, and take surfing lessons. I want to do things I've never done before."

Alex grinned again. "I'm sure I can think of a few things we haven't tried."

She rolled her eyes. "Anyway, what do you think about Hawaii? I know it's popular, but I still think it's a perfect place to spend a few weeks and not get bored."

"Hawaii it is." He raised his glass in a toast. "Be sure to take something small to wear you can get wet in. I plan on making you very, *very* wet."

"Alex!" She willed her cheeks not to heat. "Will you concentrate on actual *public* activities?"

"I was referring to snorkeling. What did you think I meant?"

Now her face was beet red, and there was no hiding it. She scooted backward, rose and collected her dishes. *Well, two can play this game.* "Obviously, I thought you were referring to sex." Walking to the sink with her dirty dishes, she heard him following suit.

"Don't worry, Isla. I don't plan on having sex with you on our honeymoon." He came up behind her at the sink.

She turned to face him, clear disbelief on her face.

"Love making, on the other hand, I plan to do a lot of," he whispered a mere breath from her lips.

She sucked in a breath and visibly shuddered. "I bought condoms today," she said a little too breathlessly. *Oh God, why did I just say that?*

He raised an eyebrow. "Taking a break from baby making, are we?" He took another step toward her, though they were already practically touching.

"I just—"

He hushed her with a finger to her lips. "Whatever you want."

Her lips became unbearably dry. She wanted to lick them, but he was still touching her there. She saw his eyes darken and knew exactly where they were headed if she didn't put a quick stop to it. "I believe you promised to spoil me."

He ran his finger down her jawline. "Suppose I drop to my knees and worship your body, starting here?" He ran his hand at the waistline of her jeans then farther down to rest on her sweet spot.

Goosebumps pricked her entire body. "Oh ..." she managed. "I was thinking retail therapy."

He left little kisses on her throat and shoulders. "I was thinking about stripping you down, coating you with expensive oils, and massaging every sore and stiff muscle in your body until you're relaxed and limber."

Her heart skipped a beat; it sounds heavenly, but she couldn't afford to be persuaded so easily. "Save it for the honeymoon, Romeo." Playfully, she pushed at his chest. "I want shoes."

It took him a moment to switch gears. His balls would not be happy with him, but he stepped backward and grinned. "As you wish, milady," he purred.

13

---

*T*hey went to the nearby mall. Isla sensibly chose some things she needed for the house, basic necessities. But she took her time sniffing candles and soaps to indulge herself in. She had been joking about the shoes, but Alex insisted. The shoe store made her feel like a kid in a candy shop. She selected a few pairs for various needs—basic ballet flats for every day, tennis shoes for working in the yard, and a pair of sexy red heels that made her feel like a sultry vixen. Alex was the perfect companion through it all, neither complaining of the time nor the cost. Isla hated to admit it, but it felt good to splurge on things she would never have sprung for on her own.

Back at her house, she put away everything and started a roast chicken in the oven for dinner. Isla and Alex sat in the rocking chairs on the front porch. Isla stared at the yard, her mind imagining things she would like to do. She wanted lilac bushes on either side of the end of the driveway and rose bushes close to the house, hostas and daylilies at the edge near the tree line.

Someone walked by with a fluffy golden retriever. Isla

gasped. She had always wanted a dog, but her father and Janice had disapproved, saying they were too messy and noisy. They preferred outdoor animals, such as horses and barn cats. Janice had owned a vicious miniature pinscher for a short time, but it was in no way the sweet family companion her friends enjoyed. Her apartment in the city had not permitted pets.

Alex had been zoned out, but Isla's gasp drew his attention, and he watched the wistful expression cross her face. He looked to see what had caused such a reaction and saw the dog. An idea brewed in his mind.

They watched the sunset, and Alex reluctantly kissed her cheek goodnight.

"You're not staying?" she asked, trying not to sound surprised.

"I've got an early morning tomorrow, and if I stay, I think what you've been avoiding all day is bound to happen."

She bit her lip, nibbling and trying to remember why she'd decided it was a bad idea in the first place.

"Say the word, Isla, and I'll stay."

DAYS LATER, Isla still regretted turning him away that night. Still a lot had been accomplished since then; she'd bought a wedding dress that fit her perfectly and was fit for a princess. Daniel was getting the treatment he needed, and worst of all, Isla got her period.

She hadn't even realized how badly she wanted to be pregnant until the possibility was gone. She'd cried alone in the bathroom, trying not to picture the little Alex she'd thought she was already carrying. But life happened, and she'd endure; now they could plan better.

Isla sat in the little coffee shop in town, awaiting Anna's presence. Since Alex was busy taking over her life, working, or wedding planning, she had a lot of free time on her hands. She was quickly falling in love with her little house. A month had passed since her father's burial, and she would be wed tomorrow. They still hadn't discussed where she would live after the wedding. Her house was not as large as Alex's, but she adored it and could easily imagine raising kids there. She shook her head, trying to block that line of thought; she had at least four years before that would become an issue. After all, a baby only took nine months, and she had five years to complete everything.

The door jingled, and she waved Anna over.

"Thank you for meeting with me," she said as Anna took a seat across from her and ordered a cappuccino and a cream cheese bagel.

"Honestly, I was surprised to receive the invitation."

"Anna, I don't want to come across as rude or prying, but I am curious as to the odds of you actually marrying my brother."

Anna raised a hand. "Trust me, you don't have to worry about that, Isla."

"I was shocked to hear the two of you had a past. I had no idea."

"It was short lived, believe me."

"Still ..." Isla shrugged.

Anna exhaled loudly. "I fell for him fast and hard, Isla— all the bad-boy charm and sex appeal. I thought I would be the one to save him. I knew he was a player, but I also knew he'd had a rough home life. I believed every lie, every story he told me. You were always the villain and he the victim. I didn't know you back then. After all, you're four years older and gorgeous. It wasn't hard to hate you."

75

Isla raised an amused eyebrow but didn't interrupt.

"You didn't know him like I did. He could be so tender when he wasn't drinking, so passionate. Did you know he bought me an overpriced, well-bred adorable Jersey calf for my birthday?" She chuckled at the memory.

Isla smiled. A pang of jealousy hit, as she wished she'd known the same boy.

"Oh, my father was pissed. 'All these Holsteins and you go out and buy a damn Jersey!' He still hates my sassy Buttercup. Always getting stuck in the damn hay feeder." She grinned. "But I'll be damned if I don't love that animal. She's been my best friend for a lot of years, and there isn't a soul on this planet who can snuggle like she can. Of course, my dad still gripes about feeding an animal who no longer produces milk, but he's just teasing. She's part of the family, even if Daniel no longer is."

"It sounds like something is still there, Anna."

"No, trust me, I still want to run him over with my car every time I see him stumble out of the bar."

"That doesn't mean anything. I'd like to hit Alex with a car, and I'm still marrying him."

Both girls laughed.

"Why is that?" Anna asked carefully.

Isla blew out a long breath. "It started as revenge. After all, I thought I'd gotten over him years ago. But coming back here, seeing his face again, hearing his voice and feeling the touch of his hand … I don't know. But I do know I was dead wrong. And now I'm afraid there's no getting over him." She frowned and sipped her coffee. "If there's even a part of you that feels the same way about Daniel—"

"No. Even with all the past bullshit aside, I could never marry a drunk."

"You left before Alex was finished reading the will. My

father is paying for Daniel to go to rehab." She thought she saw something flicker in Anna's eyes—hope?

But again, Anna shook her head. "That's not enough. A person must want to be sober."

Isla nodded in agreement. "I want to talk to you about something else. Is what Janice said about your farm true? Is it in trouble?"

"It's just a bad year. Crops didn't grow well, milk prices went down, and feed prices went up. We'll get through it. We always do."

"I get the first portion of my money tomorrow, and I want to help you." Before Anna could refuse, Isla continued. "It isn't a bribe. The money is yours whether you and Daniel work things out or not. If you don't, it's nothing more than a friendly gesture, and if you do, it's simply a gift from one sister to another."

"I always wanted a sister," Anna said with a half-smile.

"So did I, and I think you'd make a great one."

"Thank you. I'm sorry I never took the time to get to know you. I think we could have been great friends."

"I think we still can be."

The girls smiled at each other then finished their coffee and snacks and hugged goodbye.

NOT FAR AWAY, Alex visited the local pet store. He wanted to get Isla a wedding gift she wouldn't expect but would forever love. He'd seen the way she'd looked at the neighbor's dog and had heard the crack in her voice when she'd told him she'd gotten her period. Though she had tried to pass it off as no big deal, he too had felt the sting of disappointment. The thought of her swelling with his child made his heart ache in the best way possible.

So, here he was buying a puppy. The store owner recommended a goldendoodle. One of the workers had a litter of thirteen puppies that would be ready to separate from their mother in three short weeks. Alex paid a deposit for a puppy and bought everything he could think of for him or her, including a small red sweater. He decided it was best to wait and let Isla pick the one that spoke to her personally.

Grinning, he loaded the supplies into his back seat. He couldn't wait to see Isla face when he brought her to meet her gift. He had a lot to look forward to—the wedding, the honeymoon, the gift.

*F*inally, it was here. Her wedding day. Isla awoke to bright sunshine peeking through the lacy curtains. Birds chirped outside her window. The weather was mild. She couldn't have asked for a more lovely day for her wedding. If only she was getting married with all the hopes and dreams for the future that most brides felt. By nightfall, she would be Isla Renea Jones. Tonight would be her wedding night. Isla felt her body tingling in raw desire. Tonight, she could no longer deny Alex or put him off.

Alex awoke with similar thoughts. As much as he wanted Isla by his side as his wife, it wasn't enough. He wanted her to *want* to be his wife. Knowing she wouldn't be marrying him if she wasn't motivated by her disgust for her stepmother and half-brother left him feeling unsettled. He'd always felt marriage was for life, and he hated the idea that Isla was counting the days until she could leave. He reminded himself that five years gave him a lot of time to persuade her that they could have a good life together, that he would be a loving and faithful husband, as well as a doting father.

Church bells rang as Isla arrived by carriage. She'd been

waxed, bathed in rose oil, and glammed with nails, makeup, and hair all in the past few hours. If Alex didn't swoon at the sight and scent of her at the wedding, then he was sure to that night. Hidden under her wedding dress was a very sexy, very see-through negligee that made her look like a goddess.

People filled most of the seats. awaiting the union. Her hometown friends as well as a few childhood classmates had flown in. For the most part, the guests here were Alex's friends and family. Alex, she realized, had a *huge* family.

"The Wedding March" played, and she walked herself down the aisle to him. The runner was full of white rose petals that gathered as her train flowed behind her. Next to Alex stood his two brother-in-laws, and his sisters stood on her side. Though she'd only briefly met them the night before, she had instantly liked them.

Alex caught his breath at the sight of her. She was a vision in white, her dress long and flowy, her long hair in soft curls, her waist-length veil edged in lace. Her makeup was minimal and only served to enhance her natural beauty, her lips pink and glossy, her blue eyes popping from the addition of eyeliner and mascara with a little gold eyeshadow.

Isla saw Alex's tender expression. Her gaze met his, and she smiled. Regardless of what the future held, this day would be etched in her memory forever. She felt like a queen.

Isla and Alex held hands as the reverend spoke. They exchanged vows and carefully placed their wedding rings on each other's fingers. The reverend pronounced them man and wife and invited Alex to kiss his bride. Alex looked deep into her eyes and, with a mischievous expression, took her into his arms, kissing her hard and bending her into a dip, much to the delight of their wedding guests. He fully appreciated the way Isla clung to him. He stood her upright, held her hand

and raised up their joined hands while turning to face their guests.

"Ladies and gentlemen, I am pleased to introduce Mr. and Mrs. Alexander Jones!"

The guests cheered and clapped and blew bubbles as the newlyweds strode from the church and into the waiting limousine.

Isla turned to Alex. "I can't thank you enough for planning all this. It was absolutely amazing."

Alex kissed her tenderly. "My pleasure." He grinned and filled his voice with his best drawl. "But, baby, you ain't seen nothing yet!"

The reception was much less formal than the ceremony. The guests frequently clinked their glasses, indicating they wanted the couple to kiss. The food was simple but amazingly delicious. They fed each other cake and made a mess being silly. They danced their first dance. Isla laughed, watching Alex dancing the chicken dance with his nieces and nephews. Numerous family members of Alex's approached her to express their welcome to the family. Slowly, the guests trickled out. It was time to go to the room Alex had reserved for the night. Tomorrow, they would be on their way to Hawaii. Tonight, Alex had wanted to surprise her with a reservation for their wedding night.

The place enamored Isla; it wasn't the hotel she'd assumed he would choose. Instead, he'd rented a tiny cabin on a private lake and had a welcome banner hanging as they entered. The rose petals lined a path to the beautiful bedroom where large vases held lilacs on every available surface.

"Alex," she said with a sigh. "You're taking my breath away."

"Then we're even," he told her softly, following closely behind her.

She raised a finger, halting him.

Panic gripped him. He didn't think he could handle it if she denied him again, especially tonight.

But then she did something incredible; she made eye contact and slowly stripped.

His dick swelled, and his heart hammered as she shed her wedding dress—the dress she had purchased for him. "*Isla* ..." he hissed as her dress pooled at her feet, leaving her deliciously sexy in nothing but a sheer bra that had straps leading to a barely there thing.

She stepped away still in her heels and walked to him. She kissed him tenderly, teasingly, stopping him when he went to put his hands on her sides. "Uh-uh! Not yet, Mr. Jones. Good things come to those who wait." She put her hands on his shoulders and pushed him toward the bed, kissing him the whole way. When they reached the edge of the bed, she made him sit. She slowly undid his tie then tossed it aside. Next went his shirt.

When she reached for his zipper, Alex couldn't wait anymore. In one fell swoop, he grabbed her and swung her onto her back on the bed. He kissed her hard while removing his pants and boxers. He swiped at the scrap of cloth masquerading as her underwear, tearing them as he pulled them down her legs. Isla's excitement was dizzying. He buried his face in her breasts, suckling one nipple and gently biting it while pinching the other and rolling it between his thumb and forefinger.

Isla cried out from the intense pleasure.

Alex switched sides and reached for the center of her womanhood and flicked his finger across her clit.

Isla went wild, moving her hips and trying to grab him.

Alex positioned himself over her and thrust his throbbing erection into her soft, waiting body. He willed himself to go slow, to make this last, but Isla's moans and the way she moved beneath him made him lose control.

Isla screamed, throwing her head backward in ecstasy as she climaxed.

Alex shouted and felt his own release throughout every inch of his body.

Isla lay beneath Alex, panting from the intensity of her orgasm. She kissed his face and held him close, not speaking, fearing words would ruin the moment. Alex had always been an amazing lover, but tonight, he'd made her see stars. She pushed away the thought that her feelings for him and about their wedding had contributed to it. She told herself it was just good sex.

They were snuggled together so tightly, so perfectly. Isla could feel herself drifting in and out when Alex brought his lips to her ear and whispered, "I love you."

She couldn't say it back, not now while her head was still in the clouds making her insides mush. She kept her eyes closed and pretended to be asleep.

THE NEXT MORNING, Isla awoke with something very large and very ready poking her in the back. Grinning, she rolled over to see Alex smiling at her.

"Good morning, Mrs. Jones," he murmured before drawing her close and positioning her underneath him.

"Good morning, Mr. Jones," she replied with a heavy breath, spreading her legs for him.

"I'm going to get very used to waking up next to you," he assured her right before entering her.

They both gasped at the perfect fit of their bodies. They moved in slow, sweet harmony, taking time to be lazy as they touched and tasted. There was no hurry. When he felt the first pulse of her release, he let himself go and filled her with his hot seed, letting her orgasm milk every drop from him.

Afterward, they showed and washed each other's bodies, ensuring to tease as they splashed soap bubbles and used lofas in interesting places. Before the water was off, they were both fully satisfied and yet somehow still yearning for more.

They ate breakfast in the intimate dining room then packed their bags and headed to the airport. Isla already missed the cabin, but Alex promised to bring her back every anniversary.

They arrived at the island in style, and the seaside hotel staff offered them leis as they entered.

Alex had gotten them the presidential suite, so their room was more of an apartment than a room. The balcony overlooked the ocean, and the mini bar was fully stocked with champagne. A heart-shaped box of chocolates sat on the table along with an edible fruit bouquet and a cheese and sausage platter.

Snagging a chocolate-covered strawberry, she turned to Alex. "Let's put on our swimming gear and check out the beach."

"Please tell me you packed a one piece," Alex teased.

"Don't worry, darling," she said with a wink. "It's a classic red halter top bought just for you. I mean, technically yes everyone else will see it and my midriff—"

His growl cut her off. The look in his eyes had her running for cover.

She made it to the bedroom before him and slammed the door, keeping him out.

"Isla, open the door."

"I'll only be a minute, darling, and then you can get changed," she singsonged back.

His heart hammered every time she called him darling, and he hoped she never stopped.

She emerged a moment later in a one-piece suit that left her back wide open and dipped to her navel in the front with just a tiny strap holding the pieces covering her breasts together.

"You are not wearing that in public."

"Don't be such a caveman. I booked us lunch at this cute, little restaurant on the water. Get changed so we won't be late."

"You're going to lunch? In that?"

"Don't be silly." She grabbed the sheer black coverup she had bought to accompany the suit. "I'm wearing this over it." She slid it over her head and let it fall into place. "Now I'm ready, and you're still standing there." She tsked.

Reluctantly, he turned and strode to the room to change.

15

*L*unch was at a small restaurant on the beach. Alex and Isla sat on the deck, enjoying the warm breeze. Alex ordered a beer the waiter recommended from a local brewery. Isla had a piña colada. The waiter recommended the catch of the day, and both went with his suggestion. The lemon pepper sauce they paired it with was to die for, and afterward, they enjoyed a slice of sweet coconut cream pie. Isla moaned in appreciation.

She watched the trees swaying in the breeze, watched surfers trying to catch the ultimate wave and children building sandcastles. She looked inland and breathed a sigh of bliss, beholding the greenery and the mountains. This truly was paradise. When they both had finished, Alex motioned to the waiter and slipped him a few bills, telling him to keep the change and thanking him for the recommendations for their meal.

They walked off the deck onto the beach. Isla opened her beach bag, slipped out of her coverup and placed it in the bag. Alex removed his shirt, and both removed their sandals to head toward the water. Isla loved the feel of the warm sand between her toes.

Alex grinned at her. "Last one in the water is a rotten egg!" Then he took off running.

Isla shrieked and ran too. She was no match for Alex's speed, but she ran anyway, carefree and childlike. They splashed into the water, and Alex dove under, resurfaced and splashed Isla. She squealed and splashed back. They both laughed, splashing and enjoying the water. Isla gave up on not getting her hair wet and dove under herself. Several times after that, Alex picked her up and threw her into the waves. She scolded and laughed every time, trying and failing to knock him under herself. She had always loved the water, but this was her first time in the ocean. She silently vowed to herself it would not be the last.

They went back on the shore. Isla grabbed the sunscreen from her bag and applied it then asked Alex to do her back. She laid down her beach towel and relaxed to soak up some heat from the sun.

Alex sat on his own towel. He noticed other men gazing appreciatively at Isla as they walked by. It was all he could do not to tear them limb from limb for daring to lust after *his* wife. He scowled, wishing Isla had chosen a more modest swimsuit. Dammit, she was his, and he didn't want other men looking at her like a piece of meat. He wanted to make her go back to their suite, but he didn't want to spoil her fun. He would just have to keep his cool and ward off anyone who might approach her with his death stare.

The next few days had a similar feel. They took surf lessons and swam with dolphins, ate exquisite meals and sunbathed. Isla lost track of how many times they'd made love. They'd christened every piece of furniture in their suit and even did it once on the balcony in the late hours when they were sure no one else was watching.

Neither of them want the magic to end. They'd never been closer, never felt so alive as they baited then fed sharks in the wild. They went scuba diving and marveled at the rainbow fish and coral. They hiked to the old volcano and took a helicopter ride at sunset. Love was in the air, though Isla still hadn't managed to say the words back.

They ended up cutting their trip a few days short when Isla received a phone call from the rehab center. Daniel was at a difficult time in his recovery, and they asked her to come in and join him for therapy. As always, Alex was the perfect gentleman and made all the necessary arrangements, never once complaining about her family obligations. He was being the most doting husband, but something in her stomach wouldn't let her relax completely. She was forever waiting for the storm.

16

*J*sla sat in the garden with her brother and his center-provided caseworker. He looked rougher than perhaps she'd ever seen. His body wasn't taking withdrawal well and neither was his heart.

"Daniel, would you like to let your sister know why you requested to see her today?" Johnathan asked.

Daniel nodded then slowly lifted his red-rimmed eyes to hers. "Isla, I think—no, I know—you were right. I am an alcoholic. The first step is to admit I have a problem. I'm realizing I have a very big problem. I asked you here to share in this session about forgiveness." He broke eye contact and bowed his head, bringing his hands up on top and dragging it to his knees. He was so full of shame he didn't actually want to speak.

Isla sat quietly as her heart threatened to beat out of her chest. Part of her wished Alex was here to squeeze her hand, but she'd insisted on going alone, afraid what Daniel might reveal.

"I lied to you Isla," he finally croaked. Regaining eye contact, he swallowed hard. "I let you believe that prick Eddy took those pictures of you with my help. The truth is I beat the hell out of him that day in school when I found out what he did to you." He watched as pain and tears sprang to her eyes. "I lied because I didn't want you thinking someone could violate you at any time without your knowledge. I thought if you felt he had inside help, you would feel safer, that you wouldn't be scared to leave the house of horrors if you thought evil could only reach you in that house. So I lied."

They both cried, and warmth broke through a piece of the ice in her heart as she finally knew the truth; her brother had been trying to protect her.

"Thank you, Daniel, for protecting me." She sniffled.

After the much-needed breakdown and awkward hug, Daniel showed her around. He was enjoying the pool and often played water polo with other patients. He admitted the food was good, and though the therapy was hard, he felt it was working. Every day he wanted a drink, he admitted, and said he was scared to leave because the pull was so strong. Isla promised to return for another session next week before driving home.

Alex sent her an address and asked her to meet him there. She was confused when she pulled up to the tiny house with a fenced-in lawn covered in kid's toys. Still, she got out and rang the doorbell. Barking greeted her as the door opened, and Alex led her to a pen of puppies. She gasped and dropped to her knees and quickly scooped up one to nuzzle it.

"I wanted to get you a wedding gift. Pick any puppy you want, and it's yours," Alex told her affectionately.

"Oh, how can I choose when they're all so adorable!" she cooed. She had to pet every single one of them before she settled on the fat girl with a face that made her look like a bandit. "Oh, this is the one," she said, standing with her. "Look at her, Alex. This one'll be trouble."

"She's perfect."

Alex drove them to her place. He'd asked during the honeymoon if he could stay with her while his aunt's house was being remodeled and her family took over his home, and she'd agreed.

Once in the house, he showed her all the things he'd gotten for the puppy she had named Trouble. They watched her run around the yard on little legs, and Alex laughed when Isla held her against the kitchen trim to mark her height so they could watch her grow.

That night after a tender round of lovemaking, Isla turned to Alex and studied him.

He must have sensed her gaze on him because he opened his eyes and looked at her.

"Alex," she began shakily. "I've never known love. My mother died delivering me, and my father was absentee. I was never allowed to bond with Daniel and often got scolded for trying to hold him. And Janice, well, she doesn't love anyone. What I'm trying to say is what I feel for you, I've never felt for anyone, and it scares the hell out of me. I don't know what to call it."

Alex brushed a stray strand of hair from her face. His heart sang at her confession; she loved him. Even if she didn't know it yet, he finally had her confirmation, and a huge weight lifted off his chest. Had he known what she was going to say to him tonight, he would have bought her every available puppy in that place. He looked deep into her eyes and told her firmly, "I love you, Isla. I always have, and I always will."

Isla bit her lip and whispered, "I love you, Alex." She closed her eyes, afraid to see his reaction, fearing that saying the words out loud made her vulnerable. But she felt his warm, reassuring kiss. She opened her eyes and kissed him back.

Alex pulled back and smiled. "That wasn't so terrible, was it?"

Isla playfully punched him for teasing her then buried her face in his chest and drifted off.

ISLA COULDN'T KEEP the grin off her face, and it had nothing to do with all the money sitting in her bank account. It had been a week since Isla had confessed her feelings to Alex, and they'd grown so much closer.

He always found little ways of getting her to repeat the words, whether he snuck up behind her while she was washing dishes to whisper it in her ear or brought the puppy into bed with them to wake her up in the morning. He'd lean in for a kiss and whisper, "*I love you're,*" just to hear her to say it back.

They'd made love so many glorious times Isla was sure this time she had to be pregnant. She loved the routine they'd fallen into—her making him breakfast before work every morning and surprising him at the office with lunch most days, their nightly walks with little Trouble, dinner by the fireplace, and sweet hot passion between the sheets every night. Her stomach fluttered just thinking about it.

She couldn't hide her goofy grin as she drove to see Daniel. She laughed out loud, recalling the story she had to tell him. Anna had invited her to the farm and insisted on teaching her how to milk a cow. Not as easy as it looks, folks! Still, she'd washed that cow's teats and pulled until it squirted milk. She didn't even freak out when it lifted its tail and manure splattered up and into her hair. Okay, she'd shrieked a little, but she still maintained it was out of surprise.

After pulling into a parking space, she practically bounced from the car and floated on a cloud to the sign-in sheet.

*D*aniel shook his head when he saw her but smiled back. "Seeing me here really makes you that happy?" he teased then instantly regretted it as her face fell. "Relax, sis. I'm teasing. I'm sure it has a lot more to do with completing the first step of Dad's BS."

"It's a more than that, Daniel. I'm really happy. Happier than I ever thought possible." She could feel herself glowing.

Daniel jumped from his seat and desperately grabbed her hand. "Don't you fall for that con man, Isla! Remember who was there when Dad made that will. He wrote everything, implanting little ideas and using his powers of manipulation the entire time."

"No, Daniel." She shook her head.

"No, you listen to me, Isla," he demanded with a rough shake.

"Watch yourself, Goldwen," his counsel warned, nearing them.

"Isla," he whimpered. "Whose idea do you think it was to have you marry him? Who do you think chose Anna for me? Why would Dad leave my mother his fortune after he had divorced her if we failed to meet the conditions of the will? Use your head, Isla! He knew all the right buttons to push. Knew you'd never fail, that you'd do *anything* to keep that money from my mother's hands."

Isla went pale. She didn't want to have to consider this. She wanted to return to the blissful state she'd been in near minutes ago.

"Do what you have to do to win, but don't do any more. At least Father left you more than a one-bedroom house so you can maintain your marriage and raise your child under a separate roof. Under no circumstances do you let him move in with you or gain access to your bank accounts. Do you hear me, Isla?"

"I ..." She thought she might faint. "It's too late, Daniel. I deposited the money into our joint savings account."

Daniel cursed, releasing her to pace the room. "Get yourself an investor and don't tell that leech anything. You must get that money back. And remember to keep your distance. I don't want to insult you, but I'm assuming there's a chance you're already pregnant?"

She nodded.

"Good, then you're halfway there, sis. Just keep your distance."

"He's living with me."

Daniel picked up a chair and violently slammed it down.

"Warning number two, Goldwen. One more outburst and this session ends early," Jonathan warned.

"Isla, get away from him."

"His aunt is staying at his house while her house is being remodeled."

"And he'd rather live in proximity of your home than in his own gigantic one where he'd probably see no one?"

Well, when he put it like that ... "He's just being kind." She hoped more than believed at this point.

"Open your eyes, Isla. I bet there is no aunt." Goddammit, he needed a drink. How had he let this stupid sibling rivalry get so out of hand? He couldn't protect her while he was locked in this godforsaken place, and he couldn't protect her in the real world when his craving for a drink was so strong. He was stuck between a rock and a hard place, and worse, his sister was stuck between a will and self-preservation. "Isla ..." He got on his knees before her and grasped her hands. "I know you have no reason to trust me, but please look into the matters at hand. We both know Anna will never marry me. That means it's up to you to secure our father's legacy. Don't let that greedy bastard get a cent of Dad's money. He's just another Janice."

Those words repeated in Isla's brain as she drove to Alex's place. The grin had finally been ripped from her face as anxiety filled her heart. Daniel was right; she had no reason to trust him, and yet she did. Anna was also right; her brother was a different man when he was sober.

Parked in Alex's driveway, she had to concoct a plan for being here other than spying. The photographer had called to say her wedding albums were ready, so she quickly called them and asked her to meet her here. Then she'd have a nice cup of coffee with Alex's aunt, who most definitely exists, and bring the pictures home to surprise her husband. She had nothing to worry about, she told herself as got out on shaky legs.

18

*A*fter Alex's maid let her in, she filled the coffee pot in the kitchen. "Is Mrs. Jones in?" she asked the help.

"Who?"

"I'm sorry. Alex's Aunt. I guess I'm not sure what her name is actually." She laughed nervously.

"No, ma'am. No guests are currently here."

"Do you know when she'll be back?" she asked, telling herself not to freak out.

"I'm afraid I don't know what you're referring to. The house has been vacant since you and Alex officially wed."

And just like that, Isla's heart fell out of her chest and hit the floor. She calmly thanked the lady and headed to her car. The photographer caught her on her way out and sat, looking at the lies. Beautiful lies. She really wished she hadn't already agreed to host dinner for his family tonight. She'd really been looking forward to getting to know his sisters- and brothers-in-law. Now she wasn't sure if there was a point.

DRED and sheer panic filled Alex as he hung up with his head-of-household maid Emma. She'd called to see if she should prepare the guest floor for his Aunt Gloria, and he'd had to tell her no.

He hadn't wanted to tell Isla when his aunt's plans changed. She'd chosen to move in with her son and help his wife with her newest grandchild. He'd deliberately not told Isla because of how well things were going. Now he had a lot of explaining and reconciling to do.

On his way to the flower shop, his accountant called to see if he'd authorized a substantial withdrawal from his savings account, and again, he was forced to say he hadn't. Flowers wouldn't get him out of this mess.

Alex wasn't sure what he would walk into but certainly not his wife humming in an apron at the stove, frying chicken.

She turned and smiled at him. Was it his imagination, or did that smile not reach her eyes?

"Lovely," she said, regarding the flowers. "Please set them on the table."

As he gathered a vase and filled it with water, he briefly wondered if this was the calm before the storm his brothers-in-law had warned him about. And, speaking of them, he'd completely forgotten they were all coming over tonight.

"Isla, I want to discuss something with you before people start arriving."

"Don't worry, Alex. I know just what you're going to say," she cooed.

"You do?" He highly doubted it.

"Yes, and don't worry, darling. I only took my half of Daddy's money. Your half is still safe and sound in savings. "

"That's not—"

"I've been looking into the Big Brothers and Big Sisters

programs in town, and I'd really like to donate both my time and some money to the cause," she said, pulling garlic bread from the oven.

"I think that's great, but—"

"Oh, the doorbell. Go let your family in before they think I'm not the perfect little wife for you. Go!" She smacked his butt before he could reply.

This is definitely the calm before the storm, Alex thought with a knot in his stomach.

Alex went to the door and welcomed his sisters and their husbands. "Isla, you remember Claire, Mike, Sarah, and Joe."

Isla smiled brilliantly. "Of course, I do! Welcome to my humble abode." She hugged Claire and Sarah then gestured to the table. "Please, have a seat. I'm just finishing up."

Isla had prepared fried chicken, mashed potatoes with gravy, roasted asparagus, and peach cobbler. Alex's sisters praised her culinary genius, while their husbands teased him about how lucky he was to have a wife who cooks.

"Isla," Alex's older sister said partway through dinner, "did Alex ever tell you the story—"

"Shut up, Claire." Alex warned with an exasperated expression.

She grinned and waved him off. "About the time he decided to play Tarzan?"

"I swear to God, Claire, you shut up now, and I will buy you diamonds. Fat diamonds."

"Well, now I have to know," Isla said mischievously.

"*Well* ... he was eight years old and decided he needed a loincloth."

Alex groaned and shook his head.

"So he goes outside and gathers leaves to glue together. The problem is that it keeps breaking every time he tries to put the thing on. But that doesn't discourage our Alex, oh no. He finds some superglue to glue the leaves to his bare skin."

Both sisters crack up, and Isla can't help but join them.

"Is there a reason you feel the need to tell this particular embarrassing story to my wife?" Alex asks dryly while still maintaining his good humor.

"Alex, you might have a son, and she needs to know how he could turn out," Claire explained, as if saying, *duh*.

"But wait," Sarah chimed in. "That's not the best part."

"Oh, please God, if you love me, you will end this now. You still have a shot at the diamonds. Don't be Claire and blow it," he told his younger sister.

"I have to, Alex. It's the best part."

"I will kick you out of this house, Sarah Anne!"

She waved him off. "So there's our Tarzan, running around, digging holes with his hands and eating wild berries, when suddenly, he needs to use the bathroom. As you know, Tarzan does not use toilets. So there he is, squatting on our landscape rocks, when Mama comes out of the house and catches him."

Both sisters are now in hysterics, and Alex is less than amused.

"She *freaked out*! She starts yelling, 'Oh my god, you don't shit in the rocks by the house!' And our mother *never* swears," Sarah explained with a chuckle.

"Then," Claire said, jumping back in, "she turns on the hose and sprays him and yells for our dad." She imitated her mother's voice to say, "'Jeff! Jeffery, your son defecated in the yard!' All the while continuing to spray poor Alex. 'Get your butt in the house, but take off those nasty leaves.' But would they come off? No."

Everyone at the table was laughing but Alex.

"I often wonder why God gave me sisters," he muttered.

"Needless to say, he never played Tarzan again," Claire said, wiping her eyes and still laughing.

"Anything to say for yourself?" Isla asked good naturedly.

"First of all, I was seven, not eight. And second of all, that glue idea was clearly genius, because even the hose on full blast couldn't take them off."

Everyone roared again.

"How about you, Isla? Any good childhood stories?" Sarah asked.

"I don't think there's a story to top that, fictional or not." Isla smiled, though Alex noticed it didn't reach her eyes.

His sisters didn't know about Isla's childhood, and he squeezed her thigh under the table.

"However, Anna did tell me a funny joke the other day. What do you call a mother cow after it gives birth?"

Everyone frowned, thinking it over.

"De-calf-inated," she blurted on a laugh, and everyone giggled.

"Oh, please," Alex teased. "So cheesy. Here's one my six-year-old niece Piper told me. What do you call an alligator in a vest? An investigator," he said before anyone could guess, and Isla laughed.

Maybe he'd been overreacting, Alex thought, thinking of the storm he'd been preparing for. Isla was clearly fine; he'd gotten lucky.

"As long as we're telling cheesy jokes," Joe began. "How do you make a politician grow?"

"You give him Viagra!" both sisters shouted in sync, laughing.

"I was asking Isla," he scolded.

"Oh, no," Mike intervened. "I have a joke for Isla. What do lawyers name their daughter?"

"Why am I the only one getting picked on tonight?" Alex asked no one in particular.

Isla shushed him with a wink. "What?"

"Sue," he answered.

Again, everyone laughed.

"Alex darling, I'll be naming the children. We can't have little Tarzans and Sues running around, or they'll never make friends," Isla teased playfully.

Though she was having a wonderful time, Isla once again felt a blinding stab of anger at Janice for depriving her and Daniel of such a bond. But she did her best to mask it. She really liked his family, and it was clear they loved him. How lucky they all were.

After a few short hours, Alex and Isla walked their guests to the door.

"Be sure to enjoy your honeymoon phase to the fullest. Trust me, but everything changes once you have kids. Next thing you know, you can't stay out past eight p.m. or the babysitter charges double and you miss out on bedtime," his sister Sarah teased.

Isla's eyes stung at the mention of children yet again.

"Oh, I'm sorry," Sarah apologized, waving Isla off. "It's not that bad. You'll make time."

Isla wiped at tears. "It's not that. I, uh, I got my period again today."

"Oh, sweetie." Claire and Sarah both hugged her. "Don't worry. You've barely been married a month. It took me six months to get pregnant the first time. Sure, Claire got pregnant without even trying, but she's a freak of nature. Besides, now you get to continue having fun trying," Sarah said comfortingly.

"Okay, please don't talk about our sex life, Sarah," Alex

intervened and opened the door. "Out with you now. Out with all of you."

"Alright, alright. Good luck with this one, Isla," Claire teased. "Mama never thought he'd get married."

"Good night, Claire," Alex said, closing the door behind her. He reached for Isla, but she sidestepped him smoothly on her way to the kitchen, so he followed her "Why didn't you tell me?"

She simply shrugged as she loaded the dishwasher. "Nothing to say."

19

*A*lex helped rinse plates and handed them to her. When everything was done and counters were wiped down, he tried again to pull her into his arms, but again, she stepped away. He could feel his heart cracking and willed it to stay whole. So, there had been a storm brewing? Why were women so complicated, he wondered?

"I think we need to take a break from baby making," she said, scooping up Trouble to take her outside to use the bathroom before bedtime.

"Isla ..."

"It's obviously not in God's plan right now. I think it would be best if you stayed at your own house again. You know, especially since it's empty."

And there it was, the knife driven straight into his heart. "I'm not leaving you here alone, Isla. I love you."

"If you love me, you'll have no problem respecting my wishes." She walked out and shut the door in his face.

"Dammit, Isla, don't walk away from me!" He chased after her outside, wondering how the evening had gone from fun and laughter to this in the blink of an eye.

She swung around and slapped him.

"Why are you always hitting me?" He grabbed her arms and wrestled her into submission.

"Because I hate your fucking face!"

Alex had her pinned between his body and a nearby tree trunk. "Well, I suggest you get over it, baby doll, because I'm not going anywhere. Not today, not tomorrow, not ever."

"Why? I know there's no aunt, Alex." She thrashed to break free. "I also know it was your idea for my father to amend the will to trick me into marrying you."

"So, my aunt chose to stay with her son instead of me." He strained to keep her still. "That's no reason to act like a mad woman!"

"So, you admit that you lied so you could stay here!"

"Yes, I confess! I wanted to spend time with my wife," he growled.

"And do you deny knowing my father would insist I marry you or let Janice inherit?"

"Well, yes, he knew how much I love you—"

Isla slumped in his arms and wept. "That's not love, Alex. Please leave," she whispered against him.

"No," he softly replied.

She jerked in his arms and pounded her fists into his chest. "Get out!"

"No!" He threw her over his shoulder and carted her inside. He put Trouble in her kennel then brought Isla upstairs.

When he reached for her foot to remove her shoes, she stopped him and did it herself. She gathered her pajamas and turned to him in the doorway of the bathroom. "I hate you, Alex Jones," she said through tear-soaked misery.

And just like that, his heart shattered.

True to his word, Alex didn't leave that night—or any other night. He held Isla whenever she cried, and in her own self-loathing state, she didn't notice he cried right along with her. They still made love but never without a condom, and Isla was always quick to remind him it was just sex.

Though she still rose to make him breakfast, she no longer stopped by on his lunch hour. She spent more time visiting her brother Daniel and always refused to tell him what they discussed. He wasn't sure if their growing closeness was a good thing or not.

Depression overtook Isla's life. She hated herself for craving Alex the way she did and for being the one to initiate sex every single time. He didn't touch her unless she reached for him first, then he fulfilled her every need, bringing her to climax time and time again.

She cried most days, and every time her period came, she sat crumpled on the shower floor and cried as the water beat down on her even though she and Alex were no longer trying to get pregnant.

Trouble seemed to be the only one who could get close enough to her heart to make her smile. She hadn't even tried to contact the Big Brothers and Big Sisters programs like she had intended. She simply existed.

Isla sat in a lounge chair in the warm sun at one of her weekly visits with her brother. Though they had been getting along fairly well, she still wouldn't call them close. He seemed to be getting better with cravings, though he admitted to still being a long way from completing recovery.

Her mind gnawed over one particular nagging question. "Daniel, do you know why Dad and Janice divorced?" She was here for a healing session for him, but perhaps the answer would help them both.

Daniel broke eye contact and bowed his head. Why was recovery and counseling so hard? "My mother was scolding me one day for behaving badly at public functions. I was drunk and acting like an ass. She promised to punish me, and I made the off-handed remark of asking if she would make me eat from the dog food dish now that you were no longer here to do it. Dad overheard me and blew up. He blamed my mother for driving you away, never being one to take responsibility for his own actions. And that was the beginning of the end. Of course, mother always claimed it was her who walked out. Though I think we both know there was no way she willingly walked away from all that money. Thanks to a prenup, she didn't get the settlement she wanted."

Isla's face burned in shame while remembering the times she'd been so hungry she'd eaten the dinner her stepmother had thrown away into the dog food dish after the animal had eaten its fill. So much about her childhood embarrassed her even though, as a professional, she knew it wasn't her fault.

"Isla," he said, interrupting her thoughts and regaining eye contact. "I'm so sorry I let her do that to you. I'm sorry for the times I saw you eating out of that dish and never snuck you food. And most of all, I'm sorry I made fun of you for doing so." His eyes filled with shame, and she went to him.

"It's okay, Daniel," she soothed when he began to cry. "I don't blame you. You were a child."

He wrapped his arms around her, and they cried together in a very healing manner.

Isla began to feel the need for purpose in her life. She had given up her practice when she had moved back to her hometown, but she was feeling the pull to practice again. When she had thought she would soon be a mother, she had convinced herself she would not have time. Since it now seemed unlikely she would be a mother, she had scouted possibilities to practice here. She did not mention her plans to Alex.

She had looked for more things to keep her busy in the evenings to avoid Alex. She had enrolled Trouble in obedience class. She had helped Anna at the farm. She had signed up for any women-only event so Alex couldn't invite himself. She spent more days at the center with the children. One afternoon, she brought Trouble with her. Squeals of delight greeted her arrival. Most of the kids had never known the joy of having a pet—much like herself, Isla thought. She watched as the kids hugged the dog and laughed when she licked their faces. Trouble loved being the star of the show. Isla allowed the kids to take Trouble into the gym to throw the ball for her. When the puppy tired of chasing the ball, she laid on the floor. One young boy, Landon, laid down and hugged Trouble tightly, burying his face in her fur. Isla's heart melted at the sight, imagining her own child doing that exact thing someday.

Alex despaired, seeing Isla slip further from him each

day. She might be in his bed, but he was learning that proximity wasn't enough. Intimacy wasn't enough. He wanted to see her smiling at him again. He wanted to see the light in her eyes again, shining with hope for the future. He had no earthly idea how to convince her that while he had known of her father's plan to get them married, it hadn't been his idea, and his going along with it had nothing to do with the money.

Isla told him nothing of her whereabouts, and, if he asked, she replied with, "Out." He could tell how much she was hurting, and he ached to comfort her, but she wouldn't let him. He was glad to see Trouble brought her distraction from her pain. The puppy was smart and catching on fast with her training, but she was still a lovable goofball, chasing her tail and playing tug of war with her rope toys. Alex had to admit with a certain degree of envy that the canine received so much loving attention from Isla.

"GIRL, YOU LOOK TERRIBLE!" Anna told her when she was at the farm one afternoon. "You just keep losing weight, and not in a good way. What is going on with you?"

Isla shrugged, trying to downplay the living hell she was going through. "Aww, come on, Anna, you can never be too thin or too rich." Isla smiled half-heartedly.

"Lies. You can be so rich you don't know what to do with it or how to treat people. Just look at your father and Daniel. And, Isla, you are walking proof that a person can be too thin. You look ill. Now come on, out with it."

Isla told Anna about Alex lying to stay at her house and about Daniel's insistence that Alex had manipulated their father into writing his will in such a way that Isla would feel compelled to marry him against her will, while leaving Daniel with nothing.

Anna listened sympathetically. "Isla, I don't think Daniel is the person you should be listening to. I mean, I know he's in rehab, blah, blah, but I bet he's still blinded by his desperation. And, from what you said, it sounds like in the beginning, Alex's aunt staying at his house was true. Or at least the plan."

"He still should have told me. How can I trust anything he says now?" Fighting back the tears, she changed the subject. "And you should lighten up on Daniel a little. You were right about him being a different person when he's sober. And while I knew Janice was terrible to both of us, he's come out to me about some horrors he endured at her hands that I had no idea about. But he is changing, Anna."

Something flickered in Anna's eyes. Hope? Regret? She blinked and neutralized her expression. "I'm glad you two are mending your relationship. However, he better keep his distance from me. He'll find out country girls don't soon forget, and I have no shortage of manure to push him into."

Both women laughed. Isla hugged Anna and thanked her for listening before heading to the store.

*D*aniel paced the entrance, smoking a cigarette. He hadn't realized, until Isla had missed their last session how much these weekly meetings were coming to mean to him. Stomping out the finished butt, he scanned the parking lot for her car.

He popped a couple Tic Tacs; smoking, he knew, was a terrible habit. Essentially, he was trading one bad habit for another, but he needed the distraction. Every time he inhaled the tobacco, he felt a little more in control.

He breathed a sigh of relief as he saw her car turn in and park. It was raining hard, so Daniel jogged over with an umbrella before she got out, in hopes to keep her dry.

She huddled under, and together they ran for the door.

Once inside, Daniel shook the excess water off the umbrella then closed it. He helped his sister with her coat then led her to the small room where a warm fire already roared in the stone fireplace. It was one of his favorite rooms in the whole place, though he couldn't say why. The cathedral-style walls towered a good fifteen feet, with one featuring floor-to-ceiling windows.

"Nice to see you again, Isla," Johnathan greeted as she entered and sat. "First of all, I want you to know how far your brother is coming along with our therapy goals for him. I'd also like to thank you. I believe you are playing a bigger role in Daniel's recovery than you realize." He faced Daniel. "Do you think that's a fair statement?"

Daniel nodded.

Isla smiled nervously; she was still on new territory when it came to her relationship with her brother.

"I'd like to open today's session with a fun trust-building exercise." He noticed the nervous exchange the siblings shared. "Well, it's more of a game, really. It's called Pet Project. I want each of you to think of a pet project you have, something you like to do in your free time. What makes your soul sing? This could be something you've done in the past, something you're doing now, or something you've always wanted to experience. Now, I know sharing our hopes and dreams can seem scary and make us feel vulnerable, but those feelings are what make us both human and likeable. You might also be wondering why this exercise is important. Both of you were programmed as children to be seen and not heard. You were taught your wants were not important and that you job in life was to make the people around you happy at any cost. It is my job to now reprogram you, to help you see your individual importance, and to do that, I need your help." He handed each of them a clip board with a blank piece of paper and a pen. "It's important to remember that there are no wrong answers. I want each of you to section off your paper and write the numbers one, two, three."

He watched as they both did so. "Excellent. Number one is where we write the skill you love most about yourself or a skill you'd like to learn. Number two is where we write something you'd like to change about yourself. And number three is where you write about what you worry about most. Now, I want you to really think about these answers before you answer. I don't want you writing the first thing that comes to mind or the least embarrassing thing you can think of. You are family, and it is okay to share your feelings with one another."

After careful consideration, each of them wrote their answers.

Isla Jones

1- I would like to learn how to grow vegetables and start a community garden.

2- I want to learn to trust myself, my brother, husband, and my instincts.

3- I'm worried I'm in love with the wrong man and will die alone, like my father.

Daniel Goldwen

1- I want to take time to learn to play guitar and put a rhythm with the songs I've written.

2- I wish I had the ability to remain calm in stressful situations.

3- I'm worried I'll relapse when I go back to the real world. And that I'll never be good enough for my sister or Anna.

BOTH NERVOUSLY HELD their papers and avoided eye contact.

"Remember, this is a safe place. No one here will judge you." Johnathan spoke softly when he saw they were finished. "Daniel, would you please share what you wrote for number one with your sister?"

Nervously, Daniel cleared his throat. "I want to learn to play the guitar."

"Wow. I never pegged you for the musical type," Isla said in surprise.

"Yeah, well, I love to write, but Father thought it was a waste of time. I was terribly jealous of your piano lessons and, of course, as Mother said piano was for girls. So, I keep it to myself."

"I would love to hear something you wrote. And perhaps when you master guitar, we can play together some time."

Daniel nodded.

"I love to cook. I love shopping at local farmers markets, and so, for number one, I wrote I would like to learn how to plant and grow vegetables. Because I love working with children and out of the box therapy, I would like it to be a community garden. Nature has so many healing properties, as well as serving a real purpose."

"So noble," Daniel mocked. "Are you trying to make me look bad?" He watched her face fall and cursed himself. "I'm sorry. Old habits die hard, sis. I think that's something you would do well at. Would have been nice for us to have a place like that when we were kids." He half smiled at her, and she smiled weakly back. "For number two, I wish I could control my temper and my tongue better, like just now. I tend to just blurt out things, especially in stressful situations."

"And wish I was more trusting. My trust issues run so deep I don't even trust myself. I want to grow in here." She tapped above her heart. "I've kept it closed for so long, and now I fear I'll never properly open it, not to you or Alex. Even when something feels right, I don't trust my own instincts."

"I understand," Daniel said. "Between being unable to trust our own parents and abandonment issues from losing staff we loved, sometimes as frequently as six months after they're hired, it's hard to trust. Hell, I can't even trust myself to know my limits with alcohol. "

Johnathan sat back and quietly watched the exchange. These two might not know it, but a lot of families didn't make it this far in the healing process. And he had a strong feeling these two would make it out of this situation and become closer than they ever thought possible. Unlike these two, Johnathan always trusted his gut.

"What is it you're afraid of, Daniel?" Isla asked too scared to go first.

"I'm afraid I'll never leave this place." He looked down and twisted his hands. "I spend every moment of every day just wanting a fucking drink—just one shot, one beer, one taste. I'm afraid if I leave, I'll fail, and I'll never be the brother you deserve. I'll never be as good to you as you have been to me during my stay. And Isla ..." He looked up. "I'm scared to death I'll never be good enough for Anna." Blowing out a breath, he stood and paced. "God, I know even sober I'm no match for her. I know she deserves better, but I love her, Isla. And, if I get drunk again, I'll find her and tell her. I have to stay sober so I can keep myself away from her." He stopped by the window to watch the brewing storm.

"Daniel ..." Isla came up behind him and placed a hand on his back. "I know just how you feel. I've fallen in love with her too. As your sister, I think sober you *is* worthy of not only my love but hers as well. I know she still has feelings for you, even if she won't admit it—"

"Stop, Isla!" He yanked away from her. "I can't hear this. I can't know about her. Nothing, understand? I need to forget her. Please, please don't tell me about her."

Isla could only nod. Her brother had never begged for anything, and this was their trust exercise. She wouldn't let him down, wouldn't break what they were building.

"I'm afraid to end up like Dad," she confessed.

Surprised showed on Daniels face. "Isla, that will never happen. You're nothing like him. You're neither cold nor ruthless."

She shrugged. His words didn't do their job to reassure her. "I'm in love with Alex. I know you don't want to hear that, but I am. He can be so generous and so sweet. I know when I see him with his family he's not faking it. Sometimes I get jealous of the bond they share. I'm afraid I'll love him forever, and he'll leave me when the will has been fulfilled. Then I'll end up like Dad, alone and bitter." She wiped away a tear as she sniffled.

Then Daniel did something neither of them expected; he hugged her.

For once, Isla was smiling as she entered her house, loaded down with groceries. Kicking the door shut, she glimpsed Alex sitting on the living room couch with wet hair and wearing sweatpants versus his normal business suit. Her heart hammered, and when she saw he was crying, she dropped the bags and rushed to him. Kneeling before him, she cupped his face in her hand.

"Alex," she choked out in concern. "What it is? What happened?"

He didn't answer, just wrapped her in his arms, pulled her onto his lap and cried in her hair.

Despite the coldness that had existed between them for the past few months, Isla's heart broke for him. She had never seen him cry before.

"Is it one of your sisters? Did something awful happen to one of them?" She pressed herself into him as tightly as she could. The contact was as much for his comfort as it was for her.

"I just miss you so goddamn much, Isla. You never let me touch you unless it's the middle of the night, and even then, you make it as cold as possible. Do you have any idea what it feels like to love someone who doesn't even like you?"

Isla cried along with him at his words. "That has been my whole life, Alex. Loving my father who had no time or affection for the child he blamed for the loss of his wife. Loving my brother whose mother conditioned him to treat me as though I was less than human. As a young child, I yearned for the slightest hint of approval from Janice, the only mother figure I ever had in my life. And then I grew up to fall in love with a man who was more enamored with my inheritance than with me."

"Is that really what you think of me? That I'm just another person trying to marry their way into the good life?"

Isla raised an eyebrow. "Aren't you?"

Alex bit back a curse. "Isla, you've seen my house. It's bought and paid for. And, if my goal was to inherit the money, why would I go to work every day?"

Isla frowned. She hadn't thought of that.

"Isla, it's true I knew your father had planned to construct his will to persuade us to marry. It's true I didn't try to change his mind, but honestly, I don't think I could have changed his mind anyway. He was a stubborn bastard who did what he wanted, and nobody could convince him to do anything different."

"I'm having a hard time trusting your words, Alex, when I feel like you spend a lot of time manipulating me," she said on a sigh. She was still positioned on his lap and ran a finger over his stubbly chin. "I want to, but I'm scared."

He rested his forehead against hers. "Ask me anything you want, Isla, and I promise to answer truthfully."

"You tell me you love me …"

"I do, Isla." He clutched her hips, as if it were possible to bring her closer.

"Then what is it you love about me?"

"Isla," he whispered, inhaling her scent, "your soul is like a magnet to mine, constantly pulling me in. I love everything about you. I love your unbreakable spirit, your ability to laugh at all the little things in life. I love the way you light up when you're in the kitchen or playing with Trouble. I love the way you fall apart in my arms when we make love. I love the way you constantly see the best in people. You buried your father with forgiveness in your heart. You show up week after week to help your brother heal from his addiction, and you make me want to be a better man, a man who's worthy of your love. I love you so fiercely that I can't imagine my life without you ever again. Every time I see you smile at one of my nieces or nephews, I feel this longing right here." He placed her hand above his heart. "Because I know you'll make an amazing mother, and I'm just so goddamn thankful I get to be the man to share parenthood with you."

All the defenses she'd worked so hard to build shattered, and she melted in his arms. "I want that too, Alex, so bad." She kissed him desperately.

"Tell me you love me, Isla. Please. Please tell me you still love."

She did; with every fiber of her being, she loved this man —so much so that it scared her to death, and thus, she couldn't admit it out loud. "I need you," she said instead.

It wasn't what he wanted to hear, but it was a start. He gently lifted her off his lap and positioned her underneath him on the couch. Slowly, gently, he savored her body with his mouth, tasting every glorious inch of her neck and shoulders. He leaned up long enough to remove her shirt and bra so they were bare chested together.

Isla shivered from the contact; it had been a long time since Alex had been the one to kiss her first, to be the one to start their lovemaking. She moaned and withered beneath him, pulling his hair when his teeth captured her nipple, bucking wildly every time his hips thrust into her. Frantically, she shoved at his pants, needing them off him.

He helped her by kicking out of them, then slowly—so agonizingly slowly—he took her pants, kissing a path from her clit to her toes.

She was going to erupt at any moment, and he hadn't even gotten her out of her panties yet.

He teased her through the thin silk—touching, tasting, teasing, nipping until she gripped his hair and arched her back.

"Alex, please." She gasped, unable to hold still.

Patiently, he ever so slowly pulled her panties off her body, leaving scorch marks where his hands trailed on their way down. If pleasure could actually kill a person, this might very well be her last day on earth.

She opened her shaky legs for him and outstretched her arms, but he didn't come to her; he didn't put her out of her misery and enter her like she so desperately needed. For a moment, he just drank in the sight of her. Then, on a muffled moan, he buried his face between her legs.

The only thing keeping Isla on the couch was the weight of his body. The moment his tongue touched her heat, her body thrashed. He didn't rush it, didn't rush her. Instead, he slowly coaxed her body into liquid fire and blew the flames until she came on his face.

"I love you!" she screamed without conscious knowledge or thought as the orgasm ripped through her.

Alex's heart flexed, and he came up to kiss her, catch the last of her moans with his mouth. He reached for a condom, and Isla stopped him

"I want you to cum in me," she instructed breathlessly.

He swooped down and kissed her again, more hungrily this time. And then he entered her. He moved inside her achingly slow, wanting to savory every delicious moment, wanting to remember every moan, every bite of her lip and the look in her eyes as he made love to her—no, as they made love to each other.

Though she hadn't known it was possible, Isla came again, shuddering in appreciation. God, this man, her man, she loved him even through the fear. She felt so womanly, so sensual when she felt Alex quiver and release his own burning need deep inside her while whispering, "I love you," over and over again.

Isla knew she would let go of her current grudge and just enjoy the time she had with him. In the long scheme of things, five years was almost nothing at all, and the first year was already halfway over, leaving her closer to only four more years.

ISLA ENTERED HER IN-LAWS' home, which strongly resembled the White House, though possibly not quite as large. Alex had surprised her by inviting her for lunch.

"Isla, sweetheart," Mary cooed, greeting her with a hug in the foyer. "I hope you like chef salad and deviled eggs. I wanted something light."

"I enjoy them both, thank you."

"Isla, dear ..." She linked their arms and led the way to the patio where lunch was already prepared. "I must confess I brought you here under false pretenses. Though it's true I absolutely adore you and want to spend time together, I also want to pick your brain. Jeff and I are looking to do more within our community. We send checks all over the country for Greenpeace, Make-A-Wish Foundation, and cancer research. But when Alex told me what you've been up to at the local Big Brothers and Big Sisters program, as well as your work with foster kids, Jeff and I knew we had to help."

They sat at the glass table.

"Mary, that would be wonderful! There is so much hands-on you can do, such as volunteering to teach a craft or cook a meal and just as much if all you want to do is write a check! Did you know most kids are removed from their homes with nothing more than what they're wearing? We are in constant need of backpacks and school supplies, not to mention blankets, pillows, toys, jackets, and basic clothing. We'll never have enough clean socks, underwear, and bras to properly cloth all these children, not to mention a lot of these girls miss school every time they get their period due to lack of proper feminine hygiene products."

Mary smiled as she watched Isla light up with passion.

"And so many boys lack a strong male figure. If Jeff wanted to come to the center just to throw a ball or coach a spirited game of dodgeball or maybe teach them to build a birdhouse … oh, Mary, I tell you it would make their day—no, their year!" She beamed, throwing out her arms.

"You've sold me, one hundred percent. You are very inspiring, you know that? Not only will I write you a check today, but I'll also give you a list of available dates Jeff and I are free to help at the center. You can schedule us for as many or as little of the days I give you."

Islas heart sang at such wonderful news. She raised her lemonade and toasted Mary's generosity.

They finished lunch and retired to the sitting room for coffee and teacakes.

"I wanted to ask you something else, Isla … First, I want you to know Alex has never mentioned your personal life or relationship with me. However, this is a small town, and people gossip. "

Isla squirmed in her seat. She was not prepared for this conversation.

"I just want you to know that no matter the circumstances, I'm so happy to have you become part of this family. When you left all those years ago, I thought I'd lost my son forever. The light in his eyes went out, and he became so empty I feared for his health and safety. He became driven in career and nothing else. The only times I saw him smile was when his sisters married and had children. But I could tell it killed him." Mary grabbed a Kleenex and dabbed her eyes where tears sprang. "Your return brought back a hope I'd feared had left him for good. His eyes have the shine back in them, his voice has a hum I'd long ago forgotten. Isla, you've given me back my son, and I will forever be in your debt."

There were no words. Isla wanted to speak, to say something, anything, but words escaped her. Instead, she simply smiled and comfortingly squeezed Mary's hand.

23

*M*ary's words stuck with Isla through the car ride home. While Alex had gotten her to say the words again, she still didn't entirely trust him. She pondered in her mind why this was so. True, she couldn't really say she believed he was after money. She had checked the account, and he hadn't spent a cent of the money she had left him with access to. All the things he had splurged on during the honeymoon, the new SUV he had bought outright for her, claiming he wanted her in a safer vehicle, had all come from his own income as a lawyer. Clearly that hadn't been the motivation for marrying her. He had tricked her into letting him stay at her house, but he had been attentive and affectionate. If money wasn't the motivator, why had he stuck around when she had tried so hard to push him away?

Alex watched the play of emotions on her face and frowned. "Isla, if you are uncomfortable with spending your extra time with my mother, you can always schedule her volunteer hours for days you won't be there. She will be happy to still help the children whether you are there or not."

Isla eyed him with a flabbergasted expression. "What on

earth gave you that idea? I think your parents are amazing, and I can't wait to see how much their time and attention will mean to the kids."

"Okay. Well, I can tell by the look on your face that something is bothering you."

"It's not the idea of spending time with good people … Actually, I was thinking about renting an office to start seeing patients again," Isla lied.

"I can contact one of my real estate buddies and see what's available in town if you'd like."

Isla nodded. "I'd like to work with kids pro bono. Being the wife of Alex Jones and the daughter of Robert Goldwen means I don't actually need the money. Still, it is something I need to do."

ALEX'S FRIEND had found Isla a perfect office near the middle school, much better than what she had found when looking on her own. It would be the perfect location for helping kids who needed help during school hours or could stop in after school. Isla was excited to change gears; she had primarily worked with adults before.

The place was perfect for what she needed. It had two small rooms, one she could use for an office and one for sessions. It also had two bathrooms, so she planned on having one for boys and one for girls instead of having a private one to herself. A nice-sized waiting room would fit couches and vanities. Being so close to the school meant she could have students walk over afterward on dance night and help them get ready. She really wanted to teach the art of subtlety to a few select girls when it came to their makeup.

"Mary! I'm glad you made it today." Isla hugged her mother-in-law outside the children's center.

"Are you kidding? I wouldn't have missed this for anything. Let's go inside, shall we? I can't wait to meet the children you talk so much about."

Inside, several children came running. "Isla!" they yelled, hugging her tightly.

Isla's heart warmed. "Hi, guys! I'm so happy to see you. I brought someone special today. This is my husband's mother, Mary. She's very nice and very excited to get to know you all."

The children shyly but politely murmured hellos to Mary.

Isla held up her bags of groceries. "Who's up for making chocolate chip cookies?"

She was rewarded with excited cries of, "Me!"

"Great, because I'll need a lot of help! We'll see how you do, though I have complete faith. And, when it gets closer to Christmas, I'll teach you all how to make roll-out sugar cookies with cookie cutters and icing."

"You'll still be here at Christmas?" one little boy asked with a mix of hope and disbelief.

Isla knelt and placed her hands on his shoulders. "Yes, Billy, and News Years and Easter and all summer long. I don't plan on going anywhere. That's a promise." She directed her last comment to the whole room.

One of the older girls snorted, but Isla didn't take it personally. How could she when she knew the abandonment issues ran deep here? All she needed was time to prove herself, and time was one thing she had an abundance of.

In the kitchen, Isla and Mary each guided a small group of children in making chocolate chip cookies. They worked on carefully measuring the ingredients, cracking the eggs, and mixing everything together. Everyone got a chance to help in

126

one way or another. At the end, the cookies were devoured with large quantities of milk.

Mary helped some of the children with their homework.

Isla read to another group. A little girl named Violet sat on her lap, playing with Isla's hair throughout the story. When Isla was done reading, Violet had fallen asleep. Tears came to Isla's eyes. The innocence and trust of this simple act turned her insides to mush. She pulled the young girl close and stroked her hair back from her sweet face. How anyone could mistreat a child, Isla could not imagine. She vowed that her own children would never have to question whether they were loved.

"Isla, I can't thank you enough for sharing this with me," Mary told her at the end of the day. "Not only did I truly enjoy the children and their natural curiosity, but I thoroughly enjoyed spending time with you and getting to see what makes you tick."

"Thank you for coming. I really feel strongly about this place."

"That was very evident today. It's also evident that you will make a wonderful mother. You are so patient and affectionate."

Isla smiled and suppressed the urge to lay a hand on her stomach. Her period had been due two days ago, and though she prayed she was finally pregnant, she hadn't yet bought a test.

ISLA SNUGGLED under the crook of Alex's arm on the couch while they scrolled through Netflix for a movie.

"How do you feel about Thanksgiving?" Alex asked while scrolling.

"Um, I think it's great that the Pilgrims and Native Americans made peace."

"That is not what I meant," Alex said, tickling her ribs with his free hand. He loved to make her laugh and squirm against him. "I mean, how do you feel about it as a holiday party? My parents throw a big shindig every year with all my aunts, uncles, and cousins—so basically, our wedding with pumpkin pie instead of cake. I usually take the whole week off due to out-of-town family coming. A lot of them stay with my parents, and the rest bunk at my house."

"Wow, that's a lot of family."

"It is. If you'd rather do our own thing—"

"Alex, relax. I like your family. It sounds like a great time."

"Are you sure? I don't know how you typically celebrate holidays. We've never made it this far before," he said cautiously.

"Thanksgiving was never really a thing growing up. I mean, it's on a Thursday; normal people work Thursdays. Then, when I left, I spent the holidays at the local soup kitchen. We don't have one in this town. Believe me, I checked," she said with a chuckle.

"I'm sure we could find one and go in the morning together and then head to my parents," he said, putting down the remote.

"You would go with me to a soup kitchen?"

"Of course, Isla." He tilted her chin up to look at her. "I would go anywhere with you. And believe it or not, I actually enjoy helping people as well. I've been a little jealous that you've never invited me to the center."

"Oh ..." She looked away. Isla hadn't wanted him there, but it wasn't supposed to be about her; it was about the children. "Speaking of the center, they're having a

Thanksgiving fundraiser this weekend. The kids are putting on a skit, and there will be a silent auction. A lot of work has gone into it, and, if you'd like, you're welcome to accompany me."

Alex grinned at her nervous invitation. "I thought you'd never ask, Mrs. Jones." He kissed her then lightly nipped at her bottom lip before pulling away. "I wanted to ask you something else. How would you feel about staying at my house while my family is here? I know it's a lot of people, but it's a big house, and due to the staff, you'll never have to clean up or cook. I have a long list, darling, so feel free to tell me to stop at any point." He laughed. "I know Daniel is in rehab, but I also know people can get checked out for the day. My parents have agreed to a dry Thanksgiving if we'd like to pick him up. And also, my sisters are terrible cooks and have been banned from my mother's kitchen since they moved out. Now, I hate to ask, but well, it's hard to tell my mother no …"

Isla laughed at the look of dread on his face. "You know I love cooking. However, I'm not sure I'll have time to help with that and a soup kitchen and pick up Daniel if he's interested in coming." She used her fingers to add up everything.

"Isla, I have a huge family. What if we push dinner back to six p.m. and rally the troops to the soup kitchen that morning? Afterward, you can ride back with my mother and my father, and I can pick up Daniel."

"I can't." She shook her head. "This is your family's tradition. I can't ask them to rearrange it for me."

"Isla …" He rubbed her cheek. "That's what family does. We pull together, work *together*, and we love doing it." He brushed away a tear. He wanted to ring her father's neck for not showing all the love and support he and his sisters had received from their parents. No matter the time or cost, he vowed to show her what family meant.

"Okay, I'll stay at your house with you for Thanksgiving week."

"Our house, Isla," he corrected. "We have two homes." He kissed her again then refocused on the TV and settled on a Christmas movie. Holding her a little tighter, he thought of how he wanted to spoil her this Christmas, not just with gifts but with experiences.

ISLA WALKED THROUGH THE PHARMACY, grabbing her usual supplements, and couldn't help being drawn to the family planning section. She browsed the various kinds of pregnancy tests and told herself it was too soon; she was only four days late. Nonetheless, she left the store with five different pregnancy tests. She wanted to be sure. She decided to keep her purchase a secret from Alex. She hadn't told him yet that she was late. Things had been going well lately, and she didn't want to get his hopes up only to find out she was not pregnant.

She hurried home and hid the tests in the bathroom drawer where she kept her makeup and curling iron. She was certain Alex would have no reason to open that drawer and thus was unlikely to discover that she was planning to test. All the tests suggested it was best to test first thing in the morning, so she would wait until tomorrow morning. She had no idea how she would sleep tonight with such a huge question mark on her mind.

The battle in her mind between excitement at the possibility she could be carrying Alex's child and her sensibilities telling her she was only setting herself up for greater disappointment when the tests were negative plagued Isla all day.

"Isla, did something happen today? You seem distracted and not yourself," Alex commented during dinner.

"Hmm? Oh, I'm sorry. I'm just thinking about the holidays. And I'm kind of tired."

"Would you like a glass of wine? Take the edge off?"

Wine sounded amazing, but Isla knew she would never forgive herself if she was pregnant and had put her child at risk. She shook her head. "No. Thank you though."

Alex frowned. Something was bothering her, and the fact she didn't want to discuss it had him worried. Earning her trust was such a grueling process, but he knew he couldn't force her to open up to him. So instead, he took her into his arms and held her close. He kissed her forehead and looked deep into her eyes. "How about I run you a bubble bath, and you can have an early night?"

He was rewarded with a dazzling smile and a quick kiss. "Sounds like a dream come true. How did I get so lucky?"

Alex chose a bubble bath liquid labeled Relax and smelled of soft lavender. He ran the water until it was hot then plugged the tub and added the bubble bath. The soothing fragrance filled the air. He gathered the things he knew Isla would need afterward: her favorite flannel pajamas, a soft towel, her slippers. He opened the drawer to grab her blow dryer and stopped when he saw the five pregnancy tests. Suddenly, it all made sense—the weird mood, the refusal of a glass of wine. What didn't make sense was that she hadn't mentioned it. He grabbed one of the tests, and he wanted to find Isla and demand to know why she was keeping secrets from him. Then he remembered how stressed she had looked at dinner. Maybe something was wrong? He decided he was best to handle the situation with a positive attitude, lest his skittish wife decided to push him away again.

"Isla, why didn't you tell me the good news?" Alex waved the box at her.

Her expression of horror was like a punch in the gut. She clearly didn't want him to know. Isla looked at her lap. "There isn't any good news."

Alex wished the world would open up and swallow him. She had been so devastated each month when her cycle began, and he'd just reminded her of the pain. "Oh my god, Isla. I'm sorry. I saw the tests in the drawer, and I just assumed— Never mind, it doesn't matter. I'm sorry for being an ass and putting my foot in my mouth. Is that why you're upset? Because the test was negative?"

Isla shook her head. "I meant there isn't any good news *yet*. I haven't tested yet."

Alex was baffled. "Why not? How long have you suspected you might be?"

Isla lowered her eyes again. "I'm only four days late. I'm probably getting excited for nothing. The tests say it's best to test in the morning. So, I was going to test tomorrow morning." She closed her eyes. "I didn't tell you because I didn't want to get your hopes up in case I'm not pregnant."

Alex's heart melted. "Isla, I'm a grown man; you don't need to protect me. In fact, it hurts me that you have been struggling with this and kept it from me. We're supposed to be a team. We win as a team, we lose as a team, and we struggle and grow as a team. I don't want you to feel like you are alone in anything. I'm here to share in your victories and your sorrows. Tomorrow morning, I will be here when you test. Whether the tests show we'll be parents in nine months or we can keep *practicing*", he said with a gleam in his eye, "I will be here, traveling this road beside you."

Isla teared up. "Oh, Alex, you really are the best."

"I'm glad you're finally beginning to see that," he teased with a tickle.

She laughed, and he picked her up princess style and carried her to the bathroom.

"Your soak awaits, milady."

She sighed. "If only I had a nobleman to help me undress and wash my back," she said dreamily.

"Milady," he growled with his hands out, as if saying, *Hello.*

"I said nobleman, *not* caveman." She laughed.

"I think you're forgetting about the Beast. He was both noble and savage. Now strip before your king."

Isla giggled. She absolutely adored this side of him. "Well, if it's for the king. ..." She slowly removed her top.

He stepped forward, and she wiggled her finger at him.

"Oot oot, thou shalt not touch forbidden treasure."

"The king does not understand the word *no*, and he doesn't want to learn it today." He looped a finger under her black lacy bra strap and slowly dragged it down. "I do believe my queen is overdressed," he informed while freeing her breasts from their confines. "Exquisite treasures indeed." He cupped her breast and ran his thumbs back and forth over her nipples.

Isla shivered and squirmed in pleasure. How did he always know her weak points?

He bent and kissed each nibble then knelt before her to remove her bottoms.

"I see I've brought you to your knees. My evil plan is working," she said with a wicked smile.

Roughly, he yanked down her pants and undies in one fluid motion. "The king will have to punish you now." He licked a path from her inner thigh to her clit. "Such a shame," he remarked when her hips bucked, and she moaned. "Because I so wanted to worship you."

"Oh?" she asked breathlessly as he rose.

"Aye." He tilted her face, leaned in a breath away and whispered, "Now try not to scream."

24

*O*h god, her knees were like jelly. She let him turn her around and bend her over the counter. Firmly, without hurting her, he smacked her ass. She cried out in a mix of surprise and delight. He'd never once hinted at a wild side or been rough with her.

"Spread your legs," he commanded, and she obeyed. "Are you wet for your king?"

She nodded, and he smacked her other butt cheek.

"Use your words!"

"Y-Yes!" she cried out, ready for more.

Then, without preamble or warning, he thrust his entire length into her waiting heat. He gripped her hips, digging his fingers into her flush. Every time she cried out, he pulled her hair and spanked her. "I told you to be quiet!"

"I'm sorry." She gasped at the loud crack of his hand, though she wasn't sorry in the least—quit the opposite.

"Tell me," he growled, "what would you do for your king?"

"Anything," she whimpered.

He yanked his hard throbbing cock out of her, flipped her around and pushed her to her knees. "Then finish your king."

Isla opened her mouth for him and sucked greedily when he inserted himself between her lips.

Alex gripped her hair and fucked her mouth. He let her sexy moans drive him wild then cursed loudly when she gagged. When he would have pulled away, she held on, gripping his ass with her delicate hands. Alex felt the back of her throat and erupted. He came so hard and fast he could see himself dripping from her lips. He slowly eased from her.

She looked up at him, licking her lips. "Have I pleased you, milord?" she asked on a whispered smile.

"You have served your king well, Now let your king service you." Gentler now, he brought her to her feet then sat her on the counter. Pulling at her knees, he held her open to his view. "You have made your king very happy." Kneeling, he licked her sweet spot. "Now enjoy the fruits of your labor, my queen."

"As so you command, I shall do," she whimpered as he brought her to quick release.

ISLA WAS pouty by the time Alex had them nestled together in the big tub. Relaxing, she leaned back into him and closed her eyes.

"Why are you smiling, Mrs. Jones?" Alex asked while gently massaging her shoulders.

"Just thinking we should roleplay more often, *Mr. Jones*." She swiveled and scooted around to sit on his lap. She linked her arms around his neck and her legs around his back.

Alex grinned. "I think that can be arranged." Then growing serious, he kissed her tenderly and whispered, "I'm so glad you married me, Isla. I can't imagine life without you."

Isla smiled, breathed a sigh of contentment then turned around and reclined into Alex's arms, feeling so cherished and desirable. She let the heat of the bath water relax her and melt away any thoughts.

That night, nestled in bed next to Alex, Isla slept much better than she had imagined. While she still wondered what the morning would bring, she was now confident Alex would help her through.

"RISE AND SHINE, MR. JONES!" Isla said lovingly the following morning at the crack of dawn.

Alex groaned and pulled the pillow over his head. "No. It's too early. Torturer! What are you trying to do to me, woman?"

Isla poked his belly then laughed when he growled and blindly tried to grab her wrist with the pillow still over his face. "Time to get up. I have to pee!"

Alex pulled the pillow off his face and eyed her oddly, then Isla saw the realization on him and the look of hope. "Alright, alright. I'm getting up." Alex pretended to still be grumpy.

Isla insisted on using all five tests, "just to be sure."

Alex raised his eyebrows but said nothing.

She set each on the bathroom counter and set a timer on her phone. "Let's go back in our room. Otherwise, I'll just sit here, staring at them for the next ten minutes."

Alex was amused, though he felt much the same way. He hadn't realized how eager he was for him and Isla to begin their own little family, how much he wanted to show both

137

Isla and their future children what love and family is all about.

Ten minutes later, the timer beeped. Alex could see the hope and fear simultaneously in Isla's face. He kissed her and took her hand. "You won't be alone, whatever your sixty-seven tests say."

Isla burst out laughing. "Jerk," she muttered, still smiling and shaking her head as they entered the bathroom.

Pregnant. Five different tests, all with the same result. Isla shrieked and threw herself into Alex's waiting arms. "We're going to have a baby!"

He swung her around in pure glee. "You're very welcome, Mrs. Jones. I'm pretty sure we can thank last night for this," he said with a naughty wink.

Isla rolled her eyes. "That's not how it works. You can't get pregnant from swallowing."

"And yet, here you are with a baby in your belly. We'll have to remember this when we're ready for number two, because the other way just wasn't working."

Isla cracked up. God, she loved him. How could he be this funny *and* sexy as hell? She wasn't sure how, but she'd definitely won the lottery.

"Oh, honey, when you come home from work today, there will be so much baby stuff in this house you won't even know what hit your little black card!" she teased excitedly. "I'm going to pick up Anna. I promised her that she would be the first to know, then we're hitting every baby store in a hundred-mile radius *and* getting lunch!" She was practically bouncing up and down.

"Go ahead and do your worst," he said with a laugh. He retrieved his wallet and handed over his card. Despite his previous attempts, she'd never let him give her one of his own. The fact that she had both said she wanted it and to use a large sum of money made him feel so good.

Squealing, Isla took the card and skipped into the closet to get dressed.

"GIRL! I HAD BETTER BE A GODMOTHER!" Anna exclaimed, just as excited.

She and Isla were practically dancing to the car. They chatted the whole way to the mall two towns over, barely pausing long enough to breathe.

"Oh, I wish it wasn't too soon to know the gender." Anna sighed, holding up a pink tutu.

"I know, right?" Isla agreed, scanning the Daddy's Girl onesies.

"But wait," Anna sing-songed, holding up a pair of bib overalls. "Gender neutral. This kid will be a little farmer, I know it. Yes," she said to Isla's belly, "Auntie Anna will buy you a pony and a barn cat and a little Jersey calf just like mine."

Isla grinned. "Throw it in the cart."

An hour and a half later, they brought their purchases to the checkout. Isla had picked out a soft white baby blanket and a white bedside bassinet with a pink and blue ribbon. She also got a few gender-neutral outfits. Anna had forbidden her from buying up the store, stating nothing would be left for the gift registry when she threw her a baby shower.

"And before the baby shower, we'll have a gender-reveal party. They're all the rage right now," Anna assured her.

"You're such a good friend," Isla said with a hug.

"I know," Anna teased, and both girls laughed.

25

*A*lex invited his parents and sisters to dinner that night.

Isla had prepared a feast. She greeted her in-laws with hugs. She was surprised at how natural it was starting to feel to spend time with Alex's family, knowing they were as happy to see her as she was to see them. The feeling was foreign to her, though entirely a good one. As they sat around the table, enjoying good food and company, Isla met Alex's gaze and grinned.

He tapped his knife against his glass to get everyone's attention then stood. "I want to thank everyone for coming tonight. Isla and I have some special news to share." He made eye contact with his wife and grinned. "This beautiful woman who has already agreed to a lifetime with me is now going to make me a father. Isla and I are having a baby!"

Mary wept tears of joy as Claire and Sarah clapped. The men congratulated them and slapped Alex on the back. Then, as dinner finished, the men retired outside with cigars, and the woman settled in the living room, falling into the plush sofas.

"How are you feeling? Any morning sickness? When did you find out? Sorry, I'm just so happy to be getting another niece or nephew!" Claire declared.

Isla laughed. "I'm feeling good so far. We just found out this morning. No morning sickness, just a little more tired than usual and having to pee *all* the time."

Claire, Sarah, and Mary laughed.

"Just wait until he or she starts treating your bladder like a soccer ball!" Sarah teased.

Isla smiled. "I'm a little nervous about trying to make sure I'm doing everything right, but honestly, I'm looking forward to the whole experience. I can't wait to have a baby bump and show it off, even if it does come with swollen ankles and frequent peeing. I bought a few pregnancy books today, and I've read a little bit more about what is happening with my body and the baby's development."

"Just do yourself a favor, and don't Google birth videos," Sarah advised with a laugh.

"Never!" Isla agreed.

"And don't be afraid to send our dear brother to the store for pickles and ice cream at two a.m. That's his job," Claire joked.

A FEW HOURS LATER, Alex and Isla were alone, lying in bed together.

Isla turned to Alex. "Do you think the ability to be a good parent is inherited?"

"Absolutely not! I think parenting is learned from example. Good and bad. Good parents demonstrate things we want to continue with our own children—being at the soccer games, reading bedtime stories, building their self-esteem.

Bad parents teach us too. By seeing what doesn't work and what shouldn't happen, we learn not to repeat their mistakes. I have every confidence that you will be a wonderful mother, in part because you know the pain of being raised by the kind of people your father and Janice were. Because you feel strongly about their behavior, you won't do the things they did."

"Do you really believe that?" Isla's voice was shaky.

Alex placed his hands on either side of her face and looked deeply into her eyes. "Absolutely. Just think about your volunteer work at the center and your work as a therapist. Do you think your father or Janice could do what you do? Not a chance. Neither of them cared enough about other people. You're already a better dog-mom to Trouble than Janice was to you."

Hearing her name, Trouble yipped and jumped onto the bed.

Alex and Isla laughed and playfully pet the pup who was growing like a weed.

"What are you doing up here, girl?" Isla asked her naughty dog.

"Let her stay tonight," Alex said, pulling back the covers to let her under. "Pretty soon there won't be room, and we don't want her getting jealous." He pet her head before turning off the bedside lamp.

"Alex …?" Isla said quietly, gazing at him and trouble.

"Hmm?"

She smiled. "Nothing. I just really love our family."

He grinned. "Me too, sweetheart." He found her hand under the blanket and squeezed it. "I love how fast it's growing."

"Me too." Isla closed her eyes and snuggled in tight, laying one hand on Alex and the other on her belly.

26

The day of the fundraiser had arrived, and Isla awoke nauseated. She had barely cracked her eyes before she had to jump from bed and run to the toilet. Her stomach lurched violently, even after it was empty. When the heaving subsided, she lay on the cool tile floor.

Alex entered and knelt beside her, brushing her hair from her face. "Are you okay?"

"I still feel sick," Isla moaned. "How can I still feel so awful when there isn't one drop of anything left in me?"

"Because Baby Jones is making his or her presence known." Alex smirked. "With parents like us, we can't expect to produce a wallflower."

Isla grinned. "I suppose you're right. But why today? I'm supposed to be hosting the fundraiser for Big Brothers Big Sisters. Right now, I don't feel like I can even pick myself up off the floor." Isla felt strong hands scooping her from the floor. "Wait, what? You don't have to—"

"You need to lie down and rest for now. And not on the bathroom floor. The fundraiser isn't until tonight. You have all day to see if you start feeling better. If not, then we will make sure it still happens." He set her on the bed and covered her. "You need to focus on taking care of you and the baby. I will work on a backup plan. Now close your eyes. I will check on you in a bit."

Isla wanted to protest, but she was too sick. And deep down, she knew he was right. She closed her eyes and drifted off.

SHE AWOKE to the smell of toast and ginger tea.

"Hey, sleepyhead. How are you feeling?"

"Starving and nauseated at the same time."

"Claire and Sarah told me that dry toast and products with ginger were helpful for them when they were pregnant," Alex said as he presented her with a tray. "So, I made a quick trip to the store. I hope it helps."

Isla sat upright in bed and positioned the tray on her lap. "Thank you, Alex." As she ate, she became more ravenous. She forced herself to eat slowly with frequent sips of tea. But fate was not on her side. She thrust the tray at Alex and ran for the bathroom. Afterward, she cried. "I know this is normal. I know it will be worth it when the baby comes, but I feel so miserable. And I feel so guilty for letting the children down."

"Enough of that. You're allowed to feel miserable when you are sick. And you aren't letting anyone down. I called my mother while you were sleeping, and the director at the center. Mother and I will cover for you."

Isla only cried harder. "Thank you, Alex."

"That wasn't supposed to make you cry. Is this a display of those hormones my sisters warned me about?" he teased.

Her response was a scowl.

144

He laughed. "I'll take looks that could kill over tears."

Isla couldn't help but laugh.

Alex gently guided her to the bed.

"OKAY, if you're sure. I have twelve dozen sugar cookies decorated like turkeys on an orange tray in the kitchen that needs to go, along with several plates of fudge, some chocolate and some peanut butter. On the way, you'll need to stop by the farmers market pavilion. There's a guy donating all the vegetables for the veggie tray and fruit for the salad. Then I need you to go to the local market and ask for Jill. They are donating all the fruit punch tonight. At the smokehouse ask for Dan. He's donating the cheese and sausages—"

"Hold on. I need to write this down." Alex grabbed a pad of paper and pen from the nightstand.

"Once you get there, Jackie will tell you where everything goes. In the back closet is a big painting of downtown that needs to be placed in a frame that I need you to pick up from the hardware store. Just give them my name. It's already paid for. Also, I have a few jewelry store pieces in a safe in my trunk. You'll need to place both the jewelry and the painting on the silent auction tables with the other items. I realize as I'm saying it out loud how much work I'm dumping on you, but honestly, I just wanted everything to be fresh."

"It's not a problem. I'll give half the list to my mother, and we'll have everything done in no time. Now stop worrying that beautiful heart of yours. I'll take care of your center kids, and you take care of our baby." He kissed her before she could protest.

"Text me if you have any questions or forgot anything."

"I promise I'll take lots of pictures and make you proud. Now sleep."

BY THE TIME Alex had Isla's goodies loaded and half the list messaged to his mom, Isla was fast asleep. He couldn't help but be amazed by her, because he couldn't imagine doing all this on his own. He called a professional photographer who agreed to both shoot and videotape the night with her team for free. Alex didn't want Isla missing a thing, and he wanted good photos for the newspaper.

Jackie had a brief look of horror when she realized Isla wasn't coming, but thanks to Mary's years of hosting experience, her worries were soon eased. The children were bursting with energy—some excitement and some nervousness. But after being reminded to make Mrs. Jones proud, they regained focus.

Alex displayed the many items donated to the silent auction. He was completely awestruck by the painting Isla had him frame. The artist was unfamiliar but clearly brilliant. They'd painted a translucent American flag with their quiet little town depicted inside. Every business that had donated to the event was represented in the painting, and the center was right in the middle of it all.

Alex instantly fell in love with the painting and wanted to hide it and privately pay a lump sum, but that wouldn't be right. His heart was in his throat when he set it out and heard a familiar gasp.

"Oh, my stars!" his mother said, stepping beside him to admire it. "Look! There's your sister's music store."

"What did Claire donate?" Alex wondered, not seeing any instruments.

"Free music lessons for a year. Isla asked me to bid on it for her. She'd like to give it to Daniel for Christmas."

Alex's stomach twisted. She hadn't asked him for anything, hadn't even mentioned what was or wasn't donated. "Did Sarah donate?"

Mary laughed. "Free babysitting New Year's Eve."

Alex grinned; his little sister had always been clever. "I wonder why she didn't ask me to donate," Alex pondered out loud, feeling hurt.

"It's not too late." His mother placed a reassuring hand on his arm. "Surprise her."

He smiled at his mother and nodded.

"And this painting," she said, bringing his attention back to it. "I know just where I'll hang it." She smiled.

"Yes, it'll look great hanging above my fireplace. Thanks for thinking of me," he teased.

"Don't you sass your mother, Alex," Mary said sternly with a smile in her eyes.

"Just saying thank you. No sass, Mama." He turned away, needing to find Jackie and set up his own donation.

Alex explained to Jackie that not only would he like to donate a romantic weekend for two at the cabin he and Isla stayed in for their honeymoon but that he would also like to donate both property and animals for a trust farm for the children. He'd heard Isla mentioning the importance of animals with the more severely abused children and wanted to help. He also knew all the money donated tonight was to help keep the center running day to day, which didn't leave a lot of money for extras.

Jackie was delighted and confirmed his silent auction donation. They were set to open doors in twenty minutes.

Alex was blown away by the number of people who attended the fundraiser. Jackie told him this was the largest turnout the center had ever seen. Alex could see how emotional she was as she explained Isla had been the mastermind behind marketing the fundraiser to the public. She had gotten better silent auction donations, and she had hung flyers on every available space at grocery stores, gas stations, laundromats, and schools. She had also donated money to provide better catering, which resulted in the center being able to collect more money per plate and keep every cent.

The place was wall-to-wall people. Alex manuevered through the crowd, mingling with everyone. He saw many friends and clients among the guests, stopping to chat with each and thanking them for their support. He browsed through the silent auction items. The painting he wanted was a hot ticket item, and he was all too happy to make a bid he was sure would put a stop to all other bids. He also ensured to place a generous bid on the music lessons, as Isla had requested. The snacks Isla had sent were displayed for the guests to nibble while they mulled over their options.

Alex sat to enjoy his meal—a delectable plate of prime rib, creamy mashed potatoes with savory brown gravy, a warm dinner roll with honey cinnamon butter, and maple-glazed carrots. There was red wine for adults and sparkling grape juice for the kids. For dessert, there was a selection to choose from: strawberry cheesecake, rich triple-layer fudge cake, warm apple pie a la mode, or tangy lemon meringue pie. Alex chose the lemon meringue pie and immediately wished he could take a whole one home.

He went to check on the silent auction items he was bidding on. There were no further bids on the music lessons. However, much to his dismay, he had been outbid on the painting—by his own mother, no less. Well, he thought, two can play that game. He placed another bid. He couldn't say what it was about that painting that grabbed him so, but he was drawn to it, and he wanted it in his house.

The children gathered on the small stage to sing Christmas carols. Not only did they harmonize beautifully but they had several fun and uplifting songs they danced spunky too, not to mention a few that brought tears to many eyes.

Jackie took the stage again and got the children another round of applause. "Now remember, everything donated tonight directly helps these wonderful children. So please, get out your wallets, because the silent auction ends in ten short minutes. I know a lot of you here this evening have small pockets with big hearts. Please remember we are always looking for volunteers to either work with the children, help in the kitchen, or keep up the maintenance of the building. So, grab another glass of wine and enjoy the rest of the night."

Everyone clapped and Jackie left the stage.

Alex was on his way to the painting when Sarah stopped him, beaming. "Can you believe someone is paying two hundred dollars to have me babysit on a holiday?"

Alex grinned. "That's very exciting." He went to leave when Claire stopped him next.

"You realize you paid more for the lessons then I would have charged, right?" she asked with a wink.

"It's for charity, Claire. And besides, Isla wants it for her brother. You'd do the same for me, right?" He raised an eyebrow before backing away.

"Well, son, I think your wife will be very proud." Jeff clapped his son's back. "I just secured a very nice necklace for your mother I plan on hiding until next month."

"That's great, Dad. Thank you. Listen, I've gotta make my way across this room—"

"I can't let you do that, son."

And then it all clicked. It wasn't a coincidence every member of his family had stopped him; it was sabotage!

"No ..." he groaned in defeat when Jackie announced that bidding had ended and asked people with the winning bids to see Diane up front to pay for their purchases. "Awe, thanks, Mom. You shouldn't have," Alex teased, holding out his hands to take the painting.

"Well, I deserve it. It'll look great above my mantle."

"You're breaking my heart, Mother. All this time I thought you were a saint, and now I realize—"

"If you value the secrets I keep for you, you will not finish that sentence, mister."

Alex grinned at his mother. "Mastermind, mother. But I like where your mind was headed."

Mary playfully smacked her son.

Alex paid for the music lessons and a pair of earrings for Isla, along with a few other things he'd picked up for Christmas gifts. The local toy store had donated quite a few hot-ticket items. Alex chose a giant teddy bear for Sarah's daughter and a Gameboy for Claire's son. As for his own bundle of joy, he picked out a rocking horse.

Alex, his parents, and siblings, along with their spouses, stayed to help the kids and staff clean up. Before leaving, Alex made up a plate of leftovers for Isla just in case her stomach would handle it.

ISLA WAS AWAKE, sipping tea in the recliner, when Alex entered. She smiled and sighed at the photos and the video of the children's performance. She was pleasantly surprised that Alex had gotten a professional photographer; she also couldn't believe she hadn't thought of it.

"Did you buy anything?" Isla asked, nibbling on the plate of food.

"I did, but unfortunately, the one thing I really wanted, I lost to my own mother." He grimaced.

"Really? What was it?"

"The painting you had me frame. I love the way it captured the charm of our town. The colors and personality really drew me in."

Isla smiled with a raised eyebrow. "Honestly, if you like it that much, I can just paint you another."

Alex gasped. "Isla Jones! Are you telling me you painted that?"

he week of Thanksgiving arrived, and Isla had moved into Alex's house for the week. She was having a great time listening to him and his family rag on each other nonstop. And not having to clean up after herself or Trouble was a bit too alluring.

Despite her love for cooking, she'd never prepared food for such a large crowd before and was happy to pass the duty to the cook. Many of his family members had asked about the center and if they could adopt a child or two for Christmas. Isla had organized it with the coordinator and was pleased that not one child would be feeling left out this holiday season.

True to their word, the Jones family drove to the nearest soup kitchen and helped feed breakfast to the homeless. Afterward, Isla got in the car with Mary and headed to their house, and Alex and Jeff went to pick up Daniel.

Alex was nervous about being alone with Daniel; it was no secret they didn't get along. He was most grateful his father was coming along to act as a buffer.

Daniel frowned when he saw Alex instead of Isla. He

really didn't think this was a good idea, especially when he couldn't drink. Still, he mumbled a thanks and got in the vehicle.

Alex introduced the men and returned to his parents' house. When they arrived, Alex sent in his father. He wanted to have a man-to-man conversation with his brother-in-law.

"I know you don't trust me, Daniel, but I wanted to tell you that I do actually love your sister, and it has nothing to do with her bank account."

Daniel snorted. "Save the speech, Jones. I'll believe it when I see it." He opened the door and got out. "But I do hope, for your sake, that you're telling the truth, because I won't be in rehab forever," he said with a dead-eye stare. "Isla deserves better than either of us."

"At least we can agree on that."

EVERYTHING FLOWED SMOOTHLY, and more than once, one of Alex's single cousins asked Isla about her brother. Every time, she replied with the same answer. "Sorry, he's already spoken for." Despite what Daniel and Anna both claimed, Isla was holding out hope.

It was after midnight when Isla finally signed Daniel back in, much to the disapproval of the staff. "How long are you planning on staying here? It's been eight months, and I'd like you to be present when I bring your niece or nephew into the world. Not in the room, of course, but in the waiting room."

A slow smile crossed Daniel's face. "So, you're pregnant?" He pulled her into a hug. "More than halfway there, sis."

"Thanks, but it's not about Dad's will anymore. Honestly, Daniel, I love him. And I know I sound like a broken record, but I honestly think you and Anna can be just as happy. I know you're scared now, but you'll get there." She kissed his cheek before leaving.

Alex was waiting in the car when she returned from the building. He was always doing nice things to respect her privacy. He started driving back to the house.

"Alex?"

"Yes, love?"

"The baby really wants some ice cream with hot fudge," Isla said with an innocent smile.

"Let me guess—with pickles?"

"Oh, come on, Alex, you can't honestly expect our baby to be so cliche. He wants spicy tacos and ice cream."

"*He?*"

"Just a feeling, and I don't think you want Junior starting life hangry."

"Hangry?" he asked with a chuckle.

"So hungry he's angry."

"Well, we can't have that, can we?"

Alex bought the ice cream and the tacos on the way back despite the piles of leftovers shoved in the fridge at home.

They snuck in quietly so they didn't wake up their company.

Finally, Isla sighed as she fell into Alex's bed, and the fluffy blanket swallowed her whole. "Oh god, have I told you how much I love and appreciate your perfect bed? It's just so big and inviting." She moaned.

"Mrs. Jones, if you plan on getting sleep tonight, you will stop saying words like *big* and *inviting* while moaning." He climbed into bed with her.

"I can't help it. Even Junior sleeps better in this bed."

"You realize we own this entire house, right? It's ours. We can stay here whenever we want."

"*No* ..." she whined. "I'll get spoiled staying here. I can't get used to it because I'll end up missing it terribly when it's gone."

"What do you mean, when it's gone? Are you planning on torching it? Because there's no way we're selling it."

"I just ... Never mind. I misspoke," she lied, not wanting to upset him that she was still mentally preparing for things to fall apart after the five years had passed.

"You and your pregnancy brain," Alex teased.

"Should we get Christmas trees for both houses?" Isla asked a couple weeks later as they walked around the tree lot. "Or do you already have a fake one you put up every year?"

"Whatever you want, honey. I do have one with decorations, but it's not ours, and I'd like us to choose things together. I loved the traditions my family and I did every year. I'm excited to start making our own this year," Alex said smiling.

"Traditions? Like what?" she asked, inspecting a blue spruce that had caught her eye.

"Like maybe after we pick out the tree, we go ice skating and get hot cocoa or buy a special ornament to represent our journey through the year. This year, we could get a bride and groom."

"That sounds great. Then after we decorate the tree, we could put on new pajamas and make cookies to eat while watching a Christmas movie," Isla said, getting into the spirit.

"Exactly. What do you think, Junior?" Alex asked, bending to speak to Isla's belly. "Would you like some hot cocoa and cookies today? Or is it more hot tacos ice cream?"

Isla laughed at his playfulness.

In the end, they bought two trees—a five-foot tree for Islas house and a twelve-foot tree for Alex's. They bought red and gold tinsel and silver snowflakes to hang on the trees, along with the miniature bride and groom. Isla couldn't wait for Christmas; she knew exactly what to get Alex.

Christmas in the Jones family was a more intimate affair than Thanksgiving. Only immediate family attended—just her and Alex, his parents and sisters, with their families, and Daniel. They stayed up late Christmas Eve, playing games and setting out cookies and milk with the kids. By Christmas morning, Isla was bursting with excitement and so thankful her morning sickness had finally passed.

The smell of maple syrup and bacon beckoned Isla from bed. She quickly dressed and brushed her teeth before waking her husband.

"Merry Christmas, Mr. Jones," she whispered seductively, kissing and sucking at his neck.

"Mmm, Mrs. Jones, you take off those clothes and get back in this bed."

Isla chuckled. "Not a chance. We are in your parents' home, there are kids awake and ready for presents downstairs, and Junior is demanding breakfast. So, get up and get dressed, because I can't wait to see the look on your face when you open your gift from me." She dropped a quick kiss on his cheek then skipped out the room. "If you hurry, I'll show you where your dad hung the mistletoe," she sang.

Alex leaped from bed and dressed in a hurry. He hadn't seen Isla this excited since they had found out about their baby. He too had a special gift for her.

Downstairs, the adults loaded their plates and sat around

the tree while the children opened their gifts from Santa, and Sarah's husband, Joe, took pictures after drawing the short straw.

Isla was delighted by all the squeals of excitement and couldn't wait for her own children's joy in future years.

Rising, Daniel clanked his fork to his plate. "I would like to take a moment to thank you fine folks for not only opening your hearts and your home to my sister but allowing me to join you as well. I can't imagine having two holiday novices was easy."

Everyone laughed and spoke of nonsense.

"Now, before you all show me up with your beautifully wrapped gifts, I'd like Claire to join me at the piano so I can give my gift to my sister."

Isla leaned into Alex as he wrapped his arms around her in the music room.

"Before we get started, I would like to thank Claire for taking time to play with me today. Most of you don't know this but I came up with this idea about a month ago and asked Claire to help me at Thanksgiving. I'd also like to thank her husband, Mike, for listening to the song we're about to play over and over again while we practiced."

"Well, aren't you a little sneak," Isla teased while bursting with excitement.

Her brother shot her a wink. "Islas's favorite Christmas song has always been 'Let It Snow.' Pretty ironic, considering we've never had a white Christmas. But, sis, this song is for you, to the tune of your favorite childhood carol."

Claire played, and Daniel sang loudly.

"Oh, our family wasn't delightful.
In fact, they were rather frightful.

And when presents were our goal,
We got coal, we got coal, we got coal.

WE FOUND *out Santa wouldn't be stopping.*
So, with our fists we got to bopping.
How were we supposed to know?
We'd get coal, we'd get coal, we'd get coal.

WHEN WE'D FINALLY END *the night,*
How we'd hate to eat sensibly.
But then we'd sneak candy canes,
And suddenly we'd be full of glee.

WELL, *the years have come and gone.*
And now you're stuck with this song.
But as long as you love me so,
No more coal, no more coal, no more coal."

"HELP ME OUT KIDS," he said to the little ones, and they all sang: *"No more coal, no more coal, no more coal."*

Everyone laughed and clapped in delight but no one louder than Isla. She wiped a tear and hugged her brother. "Oh, I love it!" She raced to the tree and returned with her gift for him—a brand-new guitar and a gift certificate for lessons.

"Great, how are the rest of us supposed to compete with that?" Sarah teased.

Alex's niece Scarlett tugged on Islas's sleeve. "Did you really get coal for Christmas, Aunt Isla?"

Isla smiled and stroked a hand over her hair. "No, sweetheart, my brother just wanted to make me laugh." In fact, their father had paid his secretary very well to Christmas shop for Isla. She always received cashmere sweaters, Prada shoes, chenille perfume, and Gucci bags—all things she liked but nothing compared to the simple, silly song her brother wrote and had practiced just for her. Sometimes the ones who have the least to spend give the most.

In the living room, everyone else exchanged gifts. Alex presented Isla with plane tickets to visit the mountain cabin she'd inherited but had yet to visit, along with the jewelry he'd purchased from the fundraiser. And Isla gave him a painting of his childhood home during sunset with all the flowers in bloom.

"I know you liked the town painting, but I thought maybe you would like something a little more personal, something that speaks to you directly."

"Isla, you're amazing. I love it." He leaned in and kissed her.

"And honestly, Alex, these plane tickets are perfect. You are so thoughtful," she cooed.

"I have one more gift for you back at the big house. I was going to wait, but I'm terrible with anticipation. I've converted the glass gazebo into an art studio. The lighting in there is perfect, and I've heard that's important. Plus, I would love it if you painted something for Junior's room."

Isla cried then sniffled. "Damn hormones." Counting her blessings was beginning to take a lot longer.

Alex and Isla used the plane tickets and spent New Year's renovating what had once been her grandparents' cabin, then it was back to the real world of work, volunteering, and doctor's appointments.

29

*I*sla was bursting with excitement, but no matter how much she begged, Anna would not share the results of baby Jones's sex until the gender-reveal party she had planned.

Anna had Alex and Isla dressed in homemade shirts, reading: *Touchdowns or Tutus?* And giant black balloons were attached to every table.

"Everyone, make your guess before we pop the balloons and reveal the gender," Anna announced loudly.

Isla was still convinced she was having a boy and rubbed her finally visible baby bump.

"What do you think, Junior?" she asked her belly. "Will Mommy's intuition pay off?"

Daniel grinned and announced he was hoping for a niece, as he felt his family's genes were more attractive. And Mary declared it a boy. Alex and Isla held hands and counted down from ten while everyone eagerly held out their poking sticks. As soon as they shouted, "One," everyone poked their balloons, and blue glitter filled the air.

"Touchdowns it is!" Anna yelled, holding up a little baby football jersey.

Everyone shouted with excitement and hugged.

"We're having a son!" Isla threw herself into Alex's arms.

Alex bent and kissed her belly. "I can't wait to meet you, little Tarzan Junior."

Isla laughed. "I told you I'm in charge of names. I think Junior would much prefer to be called Asher Alexander Jones. I looked it up, and Asher means blessing."

"Asher … I love it. It's perfect for our little blessing."

"This is a great party, Anna," Daniel said, stopping beside her. "Pretty nice of you to do this for my sister. And what a fun way to learn I'm having a nephew."

"Well, I'm happy to do it for Isla. Turns out, she's pretty easy to love."

"I've been learning that myself." Smiling, Daniel squeezed her hand before walking away.

Anna noticed he flapped his hand afterward, as if removing her cooties. She also noticed how great his butt looked in those jeans. Biting her lower lip, she looked away only to notice other females admiring the same view. She told herself she didn't care, but the heat in her cheeks suggested otherwise.

AT THE CENTER, Mary and the kids presented Isla with a quilt they had been secretly knitting since learning the baby's gender. Isla cried into the blue fabric adorned with patches of baseballs, footballs, and tractors. The center featured Asher's name embroidered, and every child there had signed their name with fabric markers.

"You guys are seriously the best," Isla complemented as she gave out hugs.

"Will you still have time for us after the baby's born?" Erica, a thirteen-year-old and patient of Isla's, asked. In fact, she had been the first person Isla saw when her office opened.

"Not only will I continue to volunteer here and at my office but I'll also bring the baby to meet everyone. Not to mention I'll need a good babysitter once in a while."

"I'll babysit!" Little Becki volunteered excitedly. "I love babies. I like to hold them and feed them and change their yucky diapers."

Isla smiled at the seven-year-old. "Well, that sounds lovely, but babies are a lot of work, especially when they cry. I think you might do better with puppy sitting until you get a little older."

"Oh, I will, I will! I'll fed it and walk it and give it a bath," she promised very seriously.

"Perfect!"

30

*D*espite her ever-growing baby bump, Isla helped move Daniel from rehab into his new home. She'd stocked the fridge with Coca-Cola and Sprite, along with milk, eggs, cheese, bread, cereal, and ramen noodles—all the staples of a bachelor pad.

Though Isla was relieved Janice hadn't bothered to arrive, she did feel bad for Daniel. The only time his mother ever called was when she was bored and asking about his upcoming marriage. The woman had no human compassion and had sent a bottle of wine to the house. Isla quickly dumped it down the drain, and Daniel thanked her with a half-smile. Isla was thoroughly disgusted. Even if Janice didn't care about what effect the alcohol could have on Daniel's health and his life, one would think her greedy desire to get Daniel married to Anna and have him handing her a portion of the money would make her more inclined to encourage his sobriety.

Isla helped Daniel look for a job. While she could afford to support him—and was tempted to now they were on good terms—she knew her brother needed to learn the value of working for the things he wanted in life. She also knew he needed to learn to deal with the stresses of a more normal life without using alcohol as a coping mechanism. Isla was glad to see her brother had humbled enough to be proud of the house their father had left him. True, there wasn't room for overnight guests, but it was certainly not a shack. It had been tastefully remodeled, sporting a modern look and a few luxuries. Even a hot tub sat on the back deck.

Daniel applied to numerous jobs and grew frustrated that no one wanted to hire a man of his age with no work experience. Isla did her best to reassure him that something would work out eventually; the right opportunity just hadn't been found yet. She could tell he didn't entirely believe her, and honestly, she wasn't sure she believed it herself.

Claire offered Daniel a part time job at her music store as a cashier making minimum wage until he could find a more permanent position. Despite it being a pity job, Daniel accepted.

Both were surprised when Daniel proved to be a natural born salesman. The man could charm even the tightest pocket into buying something. Whether it was a popular song book or new reeds for their clarinet, he rarely had a window shopper leave empty handed.

Claire was so impressed that Daniel received his first raise after six weeks and made commission off the bigger ticket items. After ninety days, he was officially a full-time employee with health insurance.

ISLA DOUBLED OVER IN PAIN. It was 3 a.m., and the worst cramps she'd ever experienced were keeping her awake. She wanted to cry. Mentally reviewing the things she'd read in her pregnancy books, she figured it must be labor pains. Even though Junior wasn't scheduled to make his appearance for another ten days, Isla kept track of the contractions. Her son was ready and would be coming today. By 6 a.m., Isla could no longer bare it and woke up Alex, explaining she needed to go to the hospital.

He jumped out of bed so fast Isla wondered how he didn't break something. Alex dressed in record time. With his teeth barely brushed, he grabbed the hospital bag and escorted Isla to the SUV.

As they entered the hospital lobby, Isla was hit with a strong contraction and crumpled in pain.

Alex caught her, and a nurse ran to get Isla a wheelchair to wheel her to the labor and delivery unit, where the nurse confirmed Isla was in labor and asked for the details of Isla's birth plan. Isla wanted to attempt a water birth, as she had researched and thought it sounded like a natural way of delivering and would help with her goal of avoiding pain medications.

Isla settled into the bed as Alex held her hand and reminded her to breathe through her contractions like they had learned in Lamaze class. He contacted his family and Daniel to let them know Isla was in labor. He turned on the room TV to a favorite comedy show to help lighten the mood between contractions. As supportive as he was, Isla could see the stress and worry on his face.

As the day wore on, Isla progressed slowly through the labor process. She teased Alex that he shouldn't have passed his stubbornness onto their son. She sat in the birthing tub, trying to remember not to hold her breath; the pain was greater than any she had ever experienced. Her energy was depleting rapidly.

The doctor checked on her and said she was crowning.

Isla felt encouraged that it would soon be over, but the pain was relentless.

Alex had never felt so helpless and useless in his life. Watching Isla struggle through the pain, for hours, unable to help her was pure torture. He did his best to comfort and support her, but he didn't feel like he was doing enough. He wanted to demand the doctor give her something for her pain —anything to relieve her suffering—but he knew Isla had her heart set on a med-free delivery. He played soothing music from his phone, rubbed her shoulders, told her how amazing she was—anything he could think of. Somehow, when he had imagined starting a family, he had never taken the time to contemplate the process of going from baby bump to a live baby in their arms.

The doctor entered again and smiled at Isla. "Are you ready to meet your baby?"

Isla smiled weakly. "I've never been more ready for anything."

She pushed for a short time, squeezing Alex's hand with more strength than he thought she had. She grimaced and moaned, pushing with renewed energy in her desire to hold their baby.

"One more big push," the doctor encouraged.

Isla took a deep breath and pushed with everything she had.

The baby was born and made his presence known with a hearty scream.

The doctor asked Alex if he wanted to cut the cord, which he did.

They wrapped little Asher in a swaddling blanket and placed him into Isla's waiting arms. Her eyes got misty. "Oh my god, Alex, look how perfect he is! Look at our baby!"

Alex couldn't speak; he was too choked up with love for

his wife and their son. He simply put his arms around them both and kissed Isla's cheek.

ONCE MOM and baby were cleaned up, the family was invited in. The women cooed over the baby and took turns holding him.

Daniel came to his sister's side to inspect her. "Are you okay, Isla? I could hear you down the hallway, and I just kept thinking of your own mother." His voice trembled, and he was reluctant to touch the hand she offered him.

She smiled reassuringly. "I'm okay, Daniel. It was painful, that's all. I had no idea how loud I was being. I'm sorry I worried you. Come, hold my hand and meet your nephew."

Daniel sat in a bedside chair and watched as Mary placed his sister's baby in her arms.

"This is Asher. He has all ten toes and all ten fingers and is a healthy seven pounds, eight ounces," she said with such love and affection that Daniel had a moment of envy for the tiny baby already loved by his mother.

"It's nice to meet you, Asher." Daniel shook his little hand. "I'm looking forward to teaching you all the things your mother tells you no to."

Isla laughed and shook her head.

After everyone had a turn to cuddle the baby and kiss Isla, Alex shooed them out. His family needed rest, and he was looking forward to being the only one with them. He just couldn't get enough of his son and held him while Isla slept.

*E*ven after they moved back home, which Isla now referred to as The Big House, Alex ensured that either himself or a staff member catered to Isla's every need during her six-week recovery process. His heart swelled every time he watched her feed their son from her body or blow bubbles on his little belly.

Once he felt Isla was fully healed and Asher was a bit sturdier, he hired a bus to pick up the kids from the center at each of their houses on a Saturday. He then ordered enough pizza, breadsticks, and pop to feed everyone. For the most part, the girls were content to stay by Isla and Asher's sides, with Trouble jumping about. However, after about ten minutes, the boys were done, so Alex brought them to his game room. Not only did he have a pool table, air hockey, and foosball but he also had a vintage Pac-Man and Donkey Kong machine.

The day had been a hit, and he enjoyed every moment of it, as had Isla and Asher. But, as always, he was happiest when it was just the three of them.

Isla soon returned to work and her volunteering, though she cut her hours way back and brought Asher most days. Thanks to her in-laws, Anna, and Sarah, who was a stay-at-home mother, Alex and Isla had yet to feel the need to hire a nanny.

Little Asher was the perfect baby, letting anyone hold him and only fussing when he was tired or wet. The way Sarah loved on him, she was sure a baby was in her near future. Ever since her own son had hit five, she'd had a stirring for another little one to love and spoil.

And Isla couldn't help but wonder about her brother and Anna; both were exceptionally good with the baby.

"I'm not pushing you at my brother," Isla explained innocently to her friend. "All I'm saying is it would be nice if we went through it together next time. You're single, he's single. You're attractive, he's attractive."

Anna playfully smacked Isla with the couch cushion. "And all *I'm* saying is if you could wait until I'm not looking at an adorable baby with my biological clock ticking to discuss reproduction, that would be great!" She hit her with the pillow again. "And ..." she added with another smack, "it would be even more helpful if you gave up this fantasy you have of Daniel and me and set me up with one of Alex's single *attractive* relatives, that would be great. I did not find it at all funny when you introduced me to his pre-balding forty-year-old college buddy."

Isla burst into laughter. "No can do. They've all been warned to keep their distance from you."

Anna raised an eyebrow. "Oh, they've been warned, have they?"

"Scouts honor." Isla raised three fingers. "I held up a big chopping knife"—she spread her arms wide to exaggerate the size—"and I said, 'Listen here, boys, if you so much as look at my brother's girl, I will put things in this soup you do not want to eat.' And it worked."

"That's it!" Anna jumped on Isla and repeatedly bashed her with the pillows. "For the last time, I. Am. Not. Daniel's. Girl," she explained after every good blow.

Alex and Daniel entered together and stopped.

"I don't know what's going on here, but I have no objections," Alex teased.

Anna jumped off Isla, and Isla blew the hair out of her face, both girls still laughing.

"What the hell is wrong with you?" Daniel asked Anna then took a bite of food. "She just had a baby."

"Oh, please." Anna rolled her eyes. "Those are her pre-pregnancy pants. Skinny bitch had it coming. Do you want to tell him or should I?"

The men panned between the girls, and Isla shrugged, feigning innocence.

"Then you leave me no choice."

Isla pounced on her and covered her mouth with her hand. "Walk away, boys. Nothing to see here."

"And she's the one you're worried about?" Anna asked as her best friend rode her piggyback style.

"What has gotten into you?" Daniel asked, removing his sister from Anna, though he now had a chuckle in his voice. "I've never seen this side of you before."

Neither had Alex, and he found himself wanting to whisk his wife away to have his way with her. Though he often saw Isla happy and silly with the baby and the dog, he'd never seen her quite as carefree as he did now, with her hair a mess from roughhousing and her cheeks flush with wild abandonment.

Taking over for Daniel, he grabbed his wife and secretly smacked her butt, whispering in her ear, "Bad girl."

It had been a long time since he'd made love to his wife, due to the post-birth healing process. But tonight, that would change.

*A*lex awoke alone in bed. They had long since resumed staying at the smaller house where Isla felt more at home. He quietly tiptoed into the nursery, assuming Isla was feeding. He paused in the doorway, watching Isla rock their sleeping son while crying. He rushed forward and knelt beside the chair, stroking her cheek.

"Isla, my love, what is it?"

She paused her rocking and looked at him. "Please don't leave us, Alex," she choked out. "I mean, not ever. We love you, Asher and I. I want our family for a lifetime, and I know you say—"

Alex gently laid a finger on her lip and shushed her. "Sweetheart, I will never leave you, and I am so relieved to hear that you don't want me to. You and our son are the reason I wake up every morning with a smile and rush home every night." He gently took Asher and kissed him before placing him in his bed. Then he took his wife in his arms and kissed her.

"I'm so relieved to hear you say that, because it turns out it's a lot easier to get pregnant the second time."

"You're telling me that in nine months we're going to have an eighteen-month-old and a newborn?"

"Well, more like seven and a half months."

"Best. News. Ever."

"Isla," Alex said once they were back in bed. "I think we would both feel better if you stopped using this house as a security blanket and permanently moved into my house. I'm not suggesting we sell this place. Not only is it a gift from your father but we have a lot of great memories here. I think if we turned it into a well-kept guesthouse or used it as an overnight getaway for the kids at the center, you would still feel it has a purpose. I just need you to stop treating me like I'm disposable. You have no idea the amount of pain you cause me every time you throw my love for you back in my face."

Isla opened her mouth to speak then closed it. He was right. Every time he proved his love in words and actions, she held back a piece of her heart, never fully letting him in. She needed to forget the will, forget the past, and commit herself one hundred percent to her husband and their marriage.

"Okay. We'll move permanently into the big house and see how this place can be of use to the Big Brothers and Big Sisters program."

He rewarded her with a deep, gentle kiss.

"I love you, Mr. Jones," she murmured against his lips.

"I love you too, Isla Jones," he whispered back.

ONCE THEY WERE PERMANENTLY MOVED into Alex's house, Isla wondered why she had fought it for so long. She actually enjoyed having a maid clean up after them. And, as much as Isla loved cooking, it was nice to have the option of someone else doing it. With her ever-growing belly and her son toddling around, she was often exhausted by dinnertime. Morning sickness had yet to plague her this time, leading her to believe she was carrying a girl.

Alex teased Isla for her woman's intuition, but nonetheless, he brought home a soft pink blanket to pack in the new hospital bag.

Isla worked on an enchanting painting of a butterfly garden for the new baby in her beautiful art studio. She had recently finished a farm painting for Asher's room after he'd visited Anna's.

Asher had been over the moon to see all the big tractors, barn cats, and cows. True to her word, Anna had introduced him to the calves and promised he would have one of his own once he got a little older. She already had muck boots and a cowboy hat for him to wear every time he visited.

Much to Isla's dismay, Daniel started dating a fellow AA member. Though nothing seemed wrong with the lady, she was no Anna. He constantly surprised Isla by his lack of interest in his half of their father's fortune. And though she felt that was a good thing, she still believed her father had been as right about Daniel and Anna as he'd been about her and Alex.

Women's intuition told Isla that despite the current hiccup, Daniel and Anna would eventually wed. Though only time would tell …

EPILOGUE

*A*lex and Isla celebrated their five-year wedding anniversary with their kids at the cabin Isla had inherited. Asher was nearly four years old and a wonderful big brother to two-year-old Eliana. Isla sat close to the shore, watching the two of them splash in the water. She felt truly blessed to be their mother. She was so happy Alex had been right about her using her own childhood as a guide of what *not* to do. Isla had officially completed everything in her father's will, and though she was grateful to her father for bringing her and Alex back together, she still had so many unanswered questions.

Isla prepared lunch—egg salad sandwiches with fresh fruit on the side. She loved mealtimes, sitting together as a family and listening to the kids' silliness.

Alex presented Isla with a slightly aged envelope. He cleared his throat and seemed a bit uncomfortable. "This is from your father. He asked me to give this to you on our fifth wedding anniversary, if and when it arrived. I really have no idea what it says, but I feel like you should have some time to yourself to read it. I'll take the kids to the park,

176

but I'm only a phone call away if you want me to come back."

Isla nodded, staring at the envelope with her name scrawled in her father's bold handwriting. A knot formed in her stomach, unsure she wanted to know what it said.

Alex could see the pain and anxiety Isla was experiencing, and he ached to shoulder the burden for her, but he knew she needed to do this herself. He kissed her, reminding her of his love, and buckled the kids into their car seats.

Isla moved to the living room couch overlooking the lake. She sat for some time, looking at the envelope and staring unseeingly across the lake. Did she want to know what her father said? Did it really matter anymore? She and Alex were happy and raising a family, what did it matter how it started? She contemplated sacrificing the letter to their nightly campfire later. She shook her head and scolded herself for allowing a piece of paper with words written by a man who was now dead intimidate her.

Sighing, still with a feeling of dread, she opened the envelope. She took a deep breath and read.

MY DEAREST ISLA,

If you're reading this, then I have unexpectedly died as a young man. I put this plan into motion soon after realizing you wouldn't be returning home of your own accord. Turns out, you and I are more alike than either of us thought—stubborn and fiercely independent.

I hope this letter finds you well and happily married to the man I believe you would have been with all along had Daniel not told you of my attempts to meddle. I pray that by now, you have forgiven him for my mistakes, and you have the *kind of marriage that will last forever, like your mother and I had.*

I hope you can find it in your heart to forgive me for my methods of trying to get you and Alex back together. I had always hoped that someday you would return home so I could tell you Alex was a good man and how sorry I am for causing you to go separate ways.

To your credit, I must say you are the only young lady I know to leave home and not leave a trail of credit card debt in your wake. I did try to find you, but you did an excellent job of hiding so I chose to respect your wishes.

Isla, I must apologize for all the ways I failed you as a father. When I lost your mother, I was beside myself with grief. I buried myself in my work, and I told myself I was being a good father by providing you with the best things money could buy. It wasn't until you were gone that I admitted to myself that I was a coward. I didn't know how to keep myself together with you when I missed your mother so much, and when you turned out to look just like her, it only reminded me more of what I had lost. I know this was not your fault, and I realize now you didn't need things, you needed love, you needed a father who was present and made memories with you. I can't tell you how much I regret focusing on my work instead of you and Daniel.

After you left, Daniel told me off in a drunken rage one night, blaming me for allowing Janice to torture the both of you, but especially you. I had no idea the horrors you endured while I was wallowing in self-pity. I filed for divorce the next day. I couldn't stand the sight of her. And to be honest, I was forced to look in the mirror and own up to my own shortcomings and how my obsession with working had made Janice's sick games possible.

Isla, I know nothing I could ever say or do will make up

for the years I wasted that I could have spent with you. I do not deserve your forgiveness. I only hope I have corrected one of my wrongs by bringing you and Alex back together and that the money you received from me has enabled you to live a full life with him and your child or children.

Love,
Your father

ISLA CAREFULLY REFOLDED the letter after rereading it a few times. She held it to her chest and cried. After all these years, she finally got to hear the one thing she'd always longed for: her father loved her. He'd never said the words, and now all these years later, she had written proof.

She wanted to share her letter with Daniel and couldn't help but wonder what was waiting in a letter for him. Over the last few years, she'd quit meddling and trying to push the two together, but perhaps she needed to take a page from her father's book and play matchmaker.

"Hello?" Daniel answered on the first ring.

"Daniel, hey, it's Isla," she spoke softly.

"Calling to gloat, are you? How does it feel to finally be a billionaire again? You planning on moving back into Dad's house?" he teased good naturedly.

"Not quite. You still have time to earn your half. You're not an old man yet. Actually, I'm calling because I got a letter from Dad." Isla paused to let the news sink in and was met with silence.

"Dad's dead, Isla."

"I know. He must have written it before he passed. Alex wasn't allowed to give it to me until our five-year wedding anniversary. I bet he has one for you too. Would you like me to read what he wrote to you?"

179

Daniel was silent for a moment. "I can't now. I'm with the band, and we're getting ready to go on stage. But, Isla, whatever it says, I hope it brings you comfort instead of pain. I love you. We'll talk more when you get back home."

"Thank you. I love you too, and good luck on your show."

DANIEL SLIPPED his phone into his pocket and wondered yet again why his band, who all consisted of AA members, consented to playing in bars. Not only had Anna walked in, wearing jeans that were way too tight and hanging on the arm of some punk in a leather jacket, but he had this shit from his sister. What the hell had the old man been thinking?

Daniel had grown jealous of his sister's happiness over the past few years. He didn't need his father coming back from the dead to disturb that happiness. She deserved it more than anyone else he knew.

"Dan Gold Band, you're up!" the club manager shouted, bringing Daniel to the present matter at hand.

He grabbed his guitar and followed his bandmates on stage. Strumming softly, he found Anna in the crowd and made eye contact. Suddenly, he was in the mood to sing a love song.

ALEX RETURNED a little while later and laid down the children for a nap. "How are you?" he asked, sitting beside his wife on the couch and pulling her into his arms.

"I'm okay. It was everything I needed to hear. Thank you for keeping it safe for me." Isla smiled and leaned onto her husband's chest. She could honestly and truly say she was perfectly content with the way her life was turning out. "Oh, and Alex darling?"

"Hmmm?" he murmured in her hair.

"I think I might be pregnant again," she said, smiling brilliantly.

Alex pulled his wife onto his lap and removed her shirt. "I think we'd better make sure." He scooped her into his arms and jogged to the bedroom to fulfill both their needs.

THE WILL TO TRY

Did you enjoy The Billionaires Willed Wife?
Here is a sneak peek at book 2.

The Will to Try
He's got a billion reasons to wed her but his only desire is to bed her..
By H.S Howe
The Will to Try, book 2 of The Goldwen Saga.

Daniel refused to fall victim to his father's manipulation. He was just starting to mend fences with his sister Isla. The last thing he wanted was to drag Anna into their destructive web. And yet.. he'd never actually been able to forget her.

Bad boy Daniel Goldwen had been Anna's first love. His devilish good looks and smoldering eyes had completely melted her, before he broke her heart.

Now he's back in her life, seemingly a changed man. But has the bad boy grown into a dependable man? Can Anna trust he won't leave her devastated again?

Chapter one

Good God, Daniel Goldwen really was an arrogant bastard.
Anna thought as she watched him perform on stage. I mean
did the man really need to make unbreakable eye contact with
her while singing 'Shameless' by Garth Brooks? He had a
band for Pete's sake, was he even allowed to sing cover
songs?

And what the hell was wrong with her for that matter?
Not only did she know about his little side piece of ass but
she was on a date! A real date with a really attractive man that
looked damn good in a cowboy hat. But was she paying
attention to the way his arm crept around the back of her
chair? No she was too busy playing eye footsies with her ex.
Her very very bad ex..

"Do you know the lead singer?" Nate asked, trying to
bring her attention back to him.

"Hmm," she murmured barely registering the words.
"Oh, no, never met him." She answered still staring at Daniel.

"Really? Because he's looking right at you." He pointed
out.

"Oh him? He's the lead guitarist, I don't know why he is
taking vocal lead on this song. He usually sings back up. But
yeah, I know him." She said still keep her eyes on him as he
sang the love song. "He's my best friend's little brother."
Anna said as if he were no big deal.

"Ah," Nate said sounding relieved.

"Yeah," she said as if Nate had nothing to worry about.
And really he didn't, this was a first date. A step in the future.
So why was she staring so hard at her past.

Had Daniel's voice always been this deep and sexy or did
it get better with age? She wondered. And why was he
holding that microphone stand as if he were actually holding

her? And why for God's sake did she feel the need to clench her thighs and bite her lower lip while concentrating on his mouth?

Was he shameless? Hell yes he was! About loving her? That's a big fat no! So why was he pointing at her? Heads were turning, women were glaring at her and it was as if she didn't care. She couldn't look away until the song ended and he broke connection first.

Giving herself a mental shake she switched to the chair opposite Nate so she could look at him and block out her ex.

"Sorry," she said with a nervous laugh. "That was so rude. I've just never heard him sing like that before. He started a band after rehab and it's done wonders at keeping him sober." Anna chewed on her lip awkwardly.

"Hey I get it." Nate said reaching across the table to hold her fidgeting hand. "He's your best friend's brother which probably means he's like family to you. I have friends like that too. You don't have to explain yourself to me." He reassured.

Good God, this man really was a saint. And also a little clueless, but in the most adorable way possible.

"So you're a dairy farmer?" He asked moving the conversation along. She noticed he'd yet to let go of her hand and though he was a nice guy she was itching to take it away..

"Yeah, my parents and I run our family farm. Honestly that's why I don't get out very often. It's hard to find reliable workers and cows get milked twice a day whether someone calls in or not. Not to mention feeding and scraping the barns." Coolly she shifted her weight and leaned back slouching in her chair bringing her hands to her water glass.

"I get it. My grandparents had a farm until they retired. I used to spend my summers with them. All family gatherings and holidays were scheduled around the needs of the farm. I don't know how many times we were interrupted by the cows getting out, or having one in labor."

Anna laughed. "Yes, cows don't care if it's your birthday or forty degrees below zero, they do what they're going to do. So, what about you? What do you do for work?"

Nate's eyes lit up as he began describing his job as a medical researcher. It was clear to Anna that he was passionate about his work, and she was impressed while he described the promise of his current study in an experimental cancer treatment. However, she was finding it incredibly difficult to concentrate with Daniel in such close proximity. Her mind couldn't help thinking about how his snug fitting jeans had accentuated his...assets. Stop that! She mentally yelled at herself.

"That's amazing." She said drawing herself back to the conversation. "My friend Isla would love you, she's a real do gooder. But you know she's married..happily. Not that I would try to set you up with her, ha ha," she laughed nervously at herself. "Because of course, I'm on a date with you." *Oh God,* she was such an idiot. Seriously? What the hell was wrong with her? She didn't talk like this, *she made fun of* the girls who blabbed like idiots on dates.

Of course Saint Nate, who clearly should have been named Nicholas just smiled. Oh she just bet he knew he was good looking and no doubt thought he was charming his way right into her life.

"I uh, I don't date much." She said lamely. "But hey the cows don't care!" She joked. Jesus Christ, could the ground please just do her this one favor and swallow her whole?

"Me either, but hopefully we can change that."

"Right because most men want to go for airheads." *Oh shit! Was that out loud?!*

Nate laughed out loud. "Truthfully it's nice to be out with someone who isn't completely full of themselves." She relaxed a little and smiled back. "Can I buy you a drink?" He asked straightening back up in his chair.

"Oh I don't drink," she said flippantly. "I mean I can drink," she amended. "I'm not a alcoholic or anything," there was that stupid laugh again. "Oh my gosh. What I'm trying to say is that this is a AA band and I don't drink during performances out of respect."

"It's ok Anna, I like pop too."

"Oh good. Yeah me too." She blew out a breath. Her phone rang and she hoped her excitement over the distraction wasn't obvious.

"Hello?"

"Hi, it's me, just checking in." Isla said on the other line.

"What do you mean you have an emergency?"

"Um.. what's happening?" Isla asked confused.

"You know I'm on a date," Anna yell whispered. She turned in her chair and covered her phone's mouthpiece with her hand.

"Are you still talking to me?" Isla asked.

"Well of course I'm not going to leave you hanging. I don't even know how kids poop and puke at the same time but it sounds awful."

"Um yeah it does? Is that a thing that's going around? Did that med guy tell you about it?" Isla asked concerned.

"Isla! Stop yammering on, I said I'll be there. And you're damn right you owe me big." Anna yelled into the receiver.

"Ok, I get it now." Isla said as if the light finally switched on in her brain.

Daniel told himself he wasn't using his five minute break to spy on Anna and her date. It wasn't his fault she was seated between the stage and the bathroom.

He had a slight moment of panic hearing the word *emergency,* until he remembered his sister and her family were out of town. There was no way she was calling for help. This was clearly a rouse to get out of here. He couldn't help himself, suppressing a grin he pulled the phone right out of Anna's fingers.

"Isla why didn't you call me? I just talked to you thirty minutes ago and you didn't mention anything." He pretended to scold his sister.

"Oh.. hi Daniel.."

"Yes of course I'll drive her over."

"Please don't." Isla said flustered.

"Seriously I don't mind. Anything for family. Yep see ya soon." Daniel said hanging up. He frowned at the schmuck accompanying Anna. "Hi I'm Daniel. Sorry to meet this way." He held out his hand and gave him a firm handshake.

"Nate, good to meet you. You've got quite the singing voice."

"Thanks. Sorry to steal your date but it sounds urgent. Anna?" He pulled out her chair.

Anna clenched her teeth. If she had known that her escape from the horrifically awkward date would result in her leaving with Daniel Goldwen, she'd have stayed with Nate all night long. But, she couldn't back out of her lie now. And since she hadn't been honest about Daniel being her ex, she couldn't exactly justify refusing to ride with him. She gave Daniel a look of loathing, making sure that she was facing away from Nate so he wouldn't see. Then she plastered her best fake smile on her face.

"I'm so sorry, Nate, my best friend's kids are sick.

They're my godchildren, and she needs me. Thank you so much for inviting me out tonight."

"I completely understand," Nate said easily. *Why did he have to be so nice?* Anna's relief was short-lived, however, when Nate asked, "Rain check?"

Anna saw Daniel roll his eyes at Nate's obliviousness. God, why did Daniel have to be a witness in this whole situation? If he wasn't here, Anna would easily have found a gentle way to let Nate down. Hell, she might be genuinely having a good time with a man who seemed to be the real deal, had Daniel not distracted her with his wildly inappropriate performance. She saw a smirk on Daniels face, thinking he was going to get to witness her declining Nate's offer.

Anna refused to give Daniel the satisfaction. She smiled brilliantly and kissed Nate on the cheek. "How could I say no to such a gentleman? I'm so glad you asked," she lied.

She saw relief on Nate's face, and was immediately plagued by guilt. What was wrong with her? She wasn't the type to lead a guy on. She decided she would blame Daniel. He had always had a way of making her good sense go out the window.

"I have your number still. I'll text you." She said standing. Nate rose too.

"Great, I look forward to hearing from you."

Anna walked out with Daniel in tow.

"Wipe that smug look off your face. It's not what it looks like." Anna snapped.

"There's no look." Daniel said, while clearly sporting a look. "Just helping out a friend." He chuckled.

"Well thanks. Next time please mind your own business." She snapped walking to her car. "I actually really like Nate.

189

I'm just nervous dating because I haven't had sex in a while." Mother of pearl, *was that out loud?*

"I don't think I was supposed to hear that."

Anna froze. That couldn't be Nate's voice, he was still inside. And yet here he was, apparently parked right next to her..leaving at the same time.. *ok,* she changed her mind, *now is the time to swallow me whole.* Dear earth, please have mercy.

"Um.. nooo. That's not.. oh hell who am I kidding?" She threw her hands up in defeat. Nate surprised her by walking up and kissing her full on the mouth. So sweet, so nice, yet no spark. And just as quickly as it started, it was over. "That was nice," she said sighing a little. "Do you want to start this night over?"

Daniel paled. She couldn't be serious. Start the night over with this guy? Yeah he just bet this guy would love to take her home after what she'd just let slip.

"I would love too." He smiled. "How about we go somewhere quiet, get some ice cream and actually get to know each other?" He suggested.

"Anna-" Daniel said trying to intervene.

"Great idea. Is this your truck?" She asked before walking to the passenger side. "Have a good night Daniel." She smiled and winked before shutting the door on his words. Let him think what he wanted, she was just having dessert and conversation.

ACKNOWLEDGMENTS

This book was edited by Brian Paone From Scout Media. He can be found at www.scoutmediabooksmusic.com

The cover was created by Krista Ames from Covers by Kay. She can be found on Facebook. Premade covers available or order a custom cover to fit your personal needs.

Thanks to Stephanie Ruegsegger for being our Beta reader.

ABOUT THE AUTHORS

H.S Howe believes that family is everything.

H stands for Honor, yes, that's her name. Our parents didn't want us running into anyone with the same name, Bravo! What a success. Honor works as a third shift nurse and is a natural born caregiver. She loves spreading hope with her genuine smile and learning about her patients backgrounds. Her hobbies include cooking (every wonder why the cooking scenes sound so delicious? It's because she knows her way around a kitchen) bowling and playing with her children.

S stands for Samara, ah anther name that will never be found on a travel mug! Thank goodness for Etsy, they'll custom make anything! Samara is currently traveling and her only job is to work on writing, spend time with her family and explore Arizona. She loves singing, scrapbooking and of course reading.

We choose the name H.S Howe because we are sisters who writing together and love to collaborate. We are now both married but will forever be Howe girls.

f

Made in the USA
Columbia, SC
04 March 2021

33615928R00111